Awkward Tomatoes

Awkward Tomatoes

Twenty Four Short Stories

E.D.E. Bell

Detroit, Michigan

This book is dedicated to Jenn Dorohoff, who was unyieldingly encouraging back when my writing was so rough but when I needed encouragement the most, even agreeing to a "ridiculous" unicorn name, and who has been a good friend.

And to Dimitri, Ani, Stella, and Lola – May you keep reading, creating, and filling life with colorful emojis.

Dear,Readers,
     I hope you like this book.
       I made this book just for you to read.
           write me a letter.
If you know me.

- E.D.E., 1984, from her first book: *Rules are Rules*

Preface

Hello, and welcome to my first short story collection, consisting of works written between 2014 and 2020. The end of 2020 is a definite turning point (to where is TBR, but still a turning point) in my life and career, and this felt like the exact right place to draw that line for these miscellaneous tales.

I am truly proud to present this collection to you. To me, this book is more than the short stories themselves, it's also the times and themes that prompted them. Here you can see how I'd respond to a call for stories of resistance, or alternative Beatles, or of swashbuckling women and their damsels. For the record, this is not an exhaustive list of my stories, but it's the ones I've decided would be best enjoyed and/or appreciated.

And on that note of themes, I suppose I'll explain something. It's common to keep trying to sell a story if the first venue doesn't take it, and you will see that all but one of these were only submitted once. I did that for a few reasons. First, not *any* home would do. Finding anyone to publish a gem that I adore, when I am fortunate enough to have my own small press and a wonderful typesetting spouse, did not appeal to me. Second, keeping with the gem motif, many of these were cut for a specific setting. For a story built for a specific theme, moment, and requirements, I would rather publish it here, able to clarify that setting, rather than taking it out and finding somewhere, outside of that context, to place it. Third, I have an indie heart and many of these pieces would have been published somewhere but with significant changes to better suit that editor's taste. In many cases, I stand by and like the story as-is. Even if their version would be nice also, I like mine.

The stories are not edited from the original—that's not what this is—and you're absolutely welcome to skip any that don't sound appealing to you as you read through the collection. Again, this book is made both of stories I hope you like and also the interest of the stories as matched to the times and themes to which they were written. So preserving the latter was important to me. There are many shared thematic elements throughout, as there were clearly things I was trying to get out. I have clearly written through my pain as well as through my hope and through my joy, in ways that become clearer to me all the time. Also fine, as I am who I am and I've been where I've been. I hope it all works in some way.

All of this to say, I am excited to present these stories here, in this format. I enjoyed writing them—and I hope you'll enjoy reading them.

I'd also like to thank the editors and friends who assisted with these stories. I did not keep a full accounting, and I know there were many over the years so any list would be flawed, but I must certainly thank Camille Gooderham Campbell, who helped with quite a few of these, and Minerva Cerridwen and Maria Judge, who reviewed the final collection.

Another thanks: to you. If you're reading this, you are more than likely someone who appreciates my work, has supported me, has followed me. Thank you. Thank you for caring. Thank you for enjoying what I do. *I appreciate you.*

Finally, Emily, why did you call the book *Awkward Tomatoes*? Well, they are tomatoes in that people threw them back (*splat*), but also—I have a great fondness for imperfect, awkward, heirloom, colorful tomatoes. They may not fit into retail bins, and they may have a few funky spots, but they are *delicious*. And so, so, themselves.

I hope that you enjoy.

My very best,
E.D.E. Bell
November 2020

Contents

Castle Siege Adventure

I'm going to start with a piece I absolutely love, in a genre you will not know me for: romance. This was written in late 2019 for a comedic, romantic adventure collection, where one woman is a swordsmaster and one is an equally matched damsel. I wanted to make my sword story non-violent, and they said they were looking for unique settings, so I really went for both. I love this story very much.

There is another reason it has a special place in my heart. Growing up bi, it was very strictly impressed on me that I must act straight. This was planted so deeply that I didn't break through all the layers of this, even when I was out on my own, compounded by mental and social factors too complicated to get into here. Suffice it to say, in the late 90s I was often depressed and lonely. As I started writing in 2012, at that point with a spouse and three kids, my writing started and became increasingly openly queer (there is something about authentic writing that doesn't allow the soul to hide), but I hadn't said the words to anyone, except my spouse. That's complicated, as many of you will understand.

In 2019, I was essentially forced to state this identity. While I am glad now to say it, and I was working there anyway (it was right in my company name), the forcing was not nice. Soon after, when writing for this openly queer anthology, I realized that I'd set this piece subconsciously in an ambiguously alternate late 90's, one without the queerphobia I lived through during that important and difficult time in my life, and with characters who would not have to be lonely—I am sure that was a very personal pull.

I'm so proud of this swashbuckling adventure and I hope that you enjoy it.

꜓HE shared socks almost caused Maria to leave.

Yet, the woman tapping her fingernails on the clipboard outside the frayed fabric curtain had specifically called them leggings.

They looked like socks.

Reminding herself of the bills the extra cash would pay, she slid on the satiny yet somehow scratchy tubes, trying to figure out if there was even a heel. The tight fabric squeezed against her legs. "These are the largest size?" she asked.

"Yes," Clair said, though Maria had a slight question whether she was answering or talking to herself.

Resigned to her fate, Maria slid the ruffley gown over her T-shirt and wriggled her feet into what looked like the over-sized foam shoes her sister kept lined up in the mudroom. She glanced nervously at her black pants, draped over the chair. "See you soon," she whispered, before sliding the curtain open. Sliding was generous; it took a few inelegant yanks.

"Everything in the lockers; nothing's protected here—your liability," Clair ticked off, after reaching over to hook the back of the dress closed and tucking a huge tag against Maria's neck with long, sharp nails. Maria glanced over at her denim bag, slumped in the dark corner, and up at the bank of eight lockers, chunky orange-tipped keys sticking out. Where was she sup-posed to put the key? Her bag was fine.

A wig now dangled from Clair's fingers. She took it and leaned back, sliding the thin netting on.

Looking in the spotted mirror, Maria was only glad the long wavy hair disguised her enough that she shouldn't be recognized. They washed the wigs, didn't they? Or . . . sprayed them? Probably better not to think about it.

Maria spun and smiled broadly. "All set!"

"Through here," Clair directed, leading her through a series of flimsy doors into a bright pink room. A foam castle covered most of one of the walls, with gray paint sprayed over some nicked corners. "We used to stage you inside, but then we couldn't keep the kids out. So now you're here on this island—" she pointed to a green-painted bump within the scuffed blob of blue concrete "—when Zap swings down."

Zap. Alright.

"Remember, you're Princess Aria." She made a face. "Sorry, it's just everyone thinks it's *Arya* now and that's confusing and we're working it out with the board, and oh shit, the first group is already in." She looked at her watch.

"Ok," Maria said.

"Real quick." Clair pointed to a gray curtain through which a rope pulley was suspended. "Zap swings through here with the group. But then he's got a long run back to his A-point, so you need to take over fast."

"Ok."

Clair winked. "You're lucky to have the same A and B point, huh?"

"Yes."

"Now, you remember the script?"

"Sure, I'm fine. Thanks for your help."

"Great. Remember your pass-off line is—" Clair flipped through her board "—Hark, the Princess Aria! You're on your own, buccaneers!" Clair flipped the papers back. "Then you read your line and get them through the curtain by ten minutes. Room clear. Rinse and repeat."

"Ok," Maria said.

Her head was already itching by the time Clair swished out through the sequined exit curtain. Maria poked a finger under the wig to scratch it, which almost knocked the wig off so she stopped. With both hands, she wriggled the netting back into place.

She'd said the first group was in. It was, what, a fifty-minute thing? So she had no idea if the kids would be here, like, now, or in an hour?

The stocking sock thing pulled at her leg and she sat down to adjust it. Pushing her leg out, she waggled her foot in front of her and pulled at the top band.

The curtain burst open.

Dressed in all black with a tied-on eye mask and a costume looking as tight as Maria's, a figure ziplined into the room, whipping a flimsy fencing-style sword from their hand. Maria's skirt was still flipped up over her waist, and she rolled forward.

"Hark, the Princess—" The voice faltered as a group of kids ran in.

Maria sprung to her feet. "You're on your own, buccaneers."

The kids looked around, confused.

"Yes, that's right!" Zap called. "On your own. Because the Princess Aria is here!"

"I am here!" she confirmed.

Zap ran back through the curtain, disappearing, as the children looked up at Maria.

"You've found the Princess' Castle," she said. "I'd like you to join my court. Would you like to make a crown?" She gestured at the bins of foam crowns and stick-on jewels behind her, as the kids ran happily to them.

Running from station to station, she found the right colors of gems, helped peel the backings off, and then remembered to blurt out, "Oh! We've reclaimed the castle! Thank you, my royal court!" One by one, she escorted the children through the sequined curtain and toward what looked like a floating hand-scanner in the dark beyond that beeped against each of their wrists.

She looked at the timer Clair had given her, clipped to a stretchy coil loop over her wrist. If she read it right, there was only one minute left. Hurriedly, she tried to tidy the spattering of plasticky debris, but was only partway there when the curtain parted again.

"Hark, the Princess Aria! You're on your own, buccaneers!"

The line was done properly this time, yet Maria had caught the swashbuckler's eyes.

"Hi," they said.

"I got my costume on now," Maria stammered out. "Sorry about that."

"Yeah, they're awful. Mine's made for boys. I'm a girl." They, well, she, pointed to the shiny black suit, which did seem to pull in all the wrong places. "I mean, not boy gender. And I mean, I'm an adult, not a girl."

"No, it's ok, I know what you mean. I'm Maria."

"Crap!" With that, Zap ran through the curtain and Maria saw a group of kids all staring at her with quizzical gazes.

"You've found the Princess' Castle!" she managed to call out. "I'd like you to join my court. Would you like to make a crown?"

Soon, all Maria could worry about was the spray of jewel-sticker backings and two kids who both wanted the same blue crown. Maria rummaged into one of the cabinets and had just found a shrink-wrapped pack of blue glitter foam crowns when she saw her timer.

"Oh! We've reclaimed the castle! Thank you, my royal court!" She shoved a few extra blue crowns at the two warring children and it seemed to mollify them long enough to get them through the curtain. She rushed to clean up, thinking, at this rate, she was going to get fired before she got to her first break.

She heard the rumble of children. The curtain opened. Maria shut the cabinet, jumping at the harsh slam of the plywood, and rushed back to her island.

"Hark, the Princess Maria! You're on your own, buccaneers!"

"Maria?" one of the kids squealed. "It's Princess Aria!"

The other kids started to laugh. Zap threw a hand up to her mouth, and tumbled off of the zipline, dropping her sword. Maria rushed to pick it up.

"Here's your sword," she said. "My lady."

My lady? Why did she say my lady? She didn't even use that word.

The foam sword swung up against her neck, pressing gently. "I, Princess Aria, am the Swashbuckler Zap. And I'm here to rescue you and reclaim this shitty castle on your behalf."

Around them, the kids howled. Zap, seeming to realize what she'd said, whisked out of the room, and Aria, ah, Maria, whatever her name was, scrambled to make some crowns.

Ok. Got to catch up, she scolded. As she helped make crowns, she hustled to pick up the scraps and stack the new blue crowns in the blue crown dent, and that went really fast and her wrist buzzed and the kids were out of the curtain.

Maria, realizing her face was flushed and feeling sweat on her princess dress and deciding there's no way they washed these things enough, got back to her princess island on cue.

Zap was all pro this time. Swinging through the curtain, she flared her sword in a perfect zig-zag, enough that the flimsy whatever-it-was-made-of audibly swished. "Hark, the Princess Aria! You're on your own, buccaneers!"

One of the children sneezed. Zap jumped back, tripping and falling into the wall, which bowed alarmingly. Maria rushed forward to offer an arm, and pulled Zap up to her feet.

"Are you ok . . . Zap?"

"Yeah. It's Mae," she said.

"Hi. Maria."

"The Princess has a boyfriend!" one of the kids yelled out.

Maria spun on her heels. "I do not. I mean, I did, and that's not your business."

Why was she answering to some kid?

Zap, er, Mae, was staring at her quizzically. "Boyfriend?"

"Whatever works."

Whatever works?

Zap's mouth hung open and before Maria realized what she'd said, Zap was back out of the room.

"That was not your business," Maria hollered. "I don't care how funny he is, he said Janeway was pointless and what would you do with that? Now make some crowns! I mean, here, let's make some crowns."

A face poked in the curtain, long white hair swaying somehow at the same pace as the cosplay aisle fabric. "Everything alright in here?"

Maria flashed a smile. "Yes, fine. Kids, you know! Making crowns!" She looked at the children, her eyes pleading. "You're all having fun, right?"

A brief silence, then a little one piped up.

"She's the best princess *ever*."

The face retreated. The kids made crowns. Maria found the sticker roll that had tripped Zap. It must have rolled over to the doorway, damn it. The kids left. She stared at the curtain.

"Hark, the Princess Aria! You're on your own, buccaneers!"

"Oh, thank you, Swashbuckler Zap," she crowed. "You're so brave and sweet. Because of you, we're all princesses and we're going to stay here together and make some sweet, sweet, crowns."

Whatever the silly line was. Who cared.

"Are you ok?" Zap asked.

"Yes, I'm fine. And I'm sorry you tripped; it was a sticker roll. I'm supposed to be cleaning but how am I supposed to be cleaning when it's a ten-minute session and they give me ten minutes total? That makes no sense. Who scheduled this? Have they never written a schedule? Did their classes in school simultaneously stop and start at the same time? With no travel? No breaks?" She stopped, catching her breath.

"We could go out afterward. Coworker thing."

"With other coworkers?"

Mae's face froze, the mask along with it. "No. I can't stand any of them. Sorry. I'm not trying to make it weird. Was just suggesting. If you're stressed. Oh shit, I'm supposed to be on the pirate ship."

Maria widened her eyes at Mae then turned to the kids, as she heard Mae's footsteps and the swoosh of the curtain. "Welcome to the castle. Let's make crowns! Look, did you see these purple jewels? I would use these, personally. I love purple! And look at this ribbon—did you see it?"

"I went on this last week," a kid squeaked out. "And it wasn't like this at all. Also, did you notice that Swashbuckler Zap is a girl now?"

Maria stepped back. "I just noted the uh, pirating."

"She's definitely a girl," someone else said. "I like that."

Another kid agreed. "I want to be a swashbuckler, not a princess."

Maria glanced toward the exit curtain, nervous for the firing-her head to emerge again like a pizza-stage animatronic. Nothing happened. She strode toward the bins. "Ok. Swashbuckler. We can do this." Glancing around, she remembered there were no scissors. Safety reasons. Scrabbling through a drawer, she saw a pen. Jamming it into a dark purple princess crown, she carved out two rough eyes like a foam murderer. She then grabbed two blue teardrop gems, and stuck one under each eye. Like, who knew, gang tears or something. It looked great. She tied it over the kid's face.

"You're a swashbuckler," she whispered.

The other kids clapped and talked back and forth in excited tones. *Yeah, listen to that, curtain people. They love me.*

The kids filed out.

And the place was now a tornado-style mess. Maria ran about, scrambling to sweep gems and paper backings, and the carnage of her shaky foam eye sockets, and with the silent roar of a warrior, she jumped back onto the road bump island thingy. And stared at the curtain.

A familiar voice rang out.

"Hark, the Princess Aria! You're on your own, buccaneers!"

Mae spun down onto the ground, pointing the sword right at the Princess. Maria stepped forward defiantly, locking eyes with the masked swashbuckler. The kids gasped.

"You going to do something with that?" Maria let her eyes glint. "Or you just going back to your ship?"

Mae lowered the sword, her mouth twitching. "I guess you got me, Princess." She turned, and with a wave to the children, leapt through the curtain. The fabric smacked her in the face and as she whipped it to the side, Maria could hear her swearing as it sounded like several boxes spilled to the ground in the next room. Then silence.

Trying to mask her expression, she remembered there was a crowd of youth watching and waiting. She turned and raised her arms jubilantly. "You've found the Princess' Castle," she extolled. "I'd like you to join my court. Would you like to make a crown?"

Instead of the normal race to the bins, the whole group just stayed there with their eyebrows raised. "Let's make crowns!" Maria repeated.

"Yay!" a chorus rang out, and Maria, determined to keep it organized this time, made sure each one had a reasonably passable crown—and a few extra stickers—and they all filed out. On time. She was great at this. No worries. Extra cash. No more issues. Where was that swashbuckler?

"Whee!" Mae howled, and not just stepping down from her

underwhelmingly feet-from-the-ground zipline, this time she propelled forward, almost knocking right into Maria.

"Watch it, Xena!" Maria reached out and grabbed Mae's arms and they both teetered awkwardly in place, straining not to fall over. Her feet slipped against the uneven ground and she pulled herself forward.

Maria realized her face was one inch from the masked face, and she thought, how was this a kids thing with those brown eyes behind that silky black mask and Mae was breathing and apologizing, and whispered, "I'm sorry this is so awkward and I didn't mean to bang into you," and suddenly they both pulled in like magnets.

A pair of warm lips met hers and a hand glided over her costume-induced bulge of hip, and she found a tight rear with her own hand and she'd never felt such heat in her mouth and there were kids in this room so they only held close a short moment, pulling themselves apart like a tragic conclusion and stepping away.

Maria tripped over that dumb-ass island which was really just a safety hazard and she fell backward. Mae reached out and Maria grabbed her flailing arms. Together they swayed back and then over and then steadied, their faces again just nothing away, Mae's breath caressing her cheek.

The children roared in celebration. Not just a little roar, but we won the war in the movie or storming the wicked schoolteacher or endless recess was just announced and holy Banderas what was she doing?

They pulled apart, and Maria could see nothing, comprehend nothing. Then a squeak sounded behind her, and turning back, she thought she saw something poke through the curtain. A flash of silver.

Mae ran away.

Maria turned to the kids. "Let's make crowns. Here! Who wants help? Gems? Crowns? Stickers?"

"That was awesome," one whispered. "My mom fast-forwards."

"Just, come on," Maria pleaded, "be my royal court. Let's not talk about that. Got out of hand. You know. Swashbucklers. Just, uh, I'm the Princess Aria. We're making crowns. Come on, let's make some crowns."

"I'm not a princess; I'm a boss," one child declared, and Maria reached down to offer a high five.

"Never forget it," she nearly growled.

With the echo of that growl, Clair and the white-haired tattler rushed into the room, Clair waving her clipboard. "Get them out," Clair commanded, and her assistant ushered all the kids out of the room as Maria reached out her hands in silent protest. One of the kids lingered in the curtain, waving back. Maria smiled, and waved. "I hope you had fun," she whispered. Then the child was gone.

Clair's face flashed beet red. "This. Is. A. Children's. Event. You are—"

Just then, Mae pushed back through the swashbuckler's curtain, her sword dragging at her side.

"Yes, we know, Clair," Mae stammered out. "Sorry, we just got some play-acting in. New cast. Figuring things out. The kids were really enjoying it. We'll go back to the script now. Totally straight."

Realizing what she'd said, Mae grimaced and swung the

sword across her chest like a salute. As her eyes met Maria's, they both burst into laughter.

"You are fired!" Clair shouted. *"Both of you."*

A punch to her gut. As much as Maria wanted to laugh, she'd needed that money. Even a weekend's worth would have helped.

But Mae had raised her sword and was striding forward. What was she doing?

"Fired? Then you owe us a week's pay."

"I owe you?" Clair turned and pointed at Maria. "She just started! Like, right now."

"But she signed a contract. There's a copy locked in her locker; I know it. Just like I've got mine. Contract says in case of termination, we're owed 40 hours pay. I read it."

"Negated! There's a code of conduct."

Mae stepped forward again, her sword still pointed in front of her. "There isn't. Show me."

Clair huffed. Then again. "Fine. You people make nothing, anyway. Here. She pulled out a pouch and counted a series of bills down onto the crown-making table, dramatically whisking them into two piles. "Take this if I'll never see you again. Lew can run *both* of your pieces. Better than you."

Maria intended to slide the cash into a pocket then realized the silky nightmare she was wearing had none. Mae had hovered hers over the black suit with the same dilemma. Again, they both laughed, trying to stifle it in Clair's presence but completely failing.

Before they enraged the woman further, they hurried back out through the curtain. "This way to the dressing room," Mae said.

"Good, my stuff is all there. I wasn't sure I'd remember." They'd really made this place a maze.

"So . . . where you want to go?" Mae asked, with Clair out of hearing.

"I'm a vegan." Maria stammered, knowing the date-killer that was. "And I'm kind of broke."

"You're kidding."

Maria's heart—

"Me too! I know an Ethiopian strip mall place. They take care of me. After that," Mae started to say. But there was only one dressing booth in the women's locker area, and about ten seconds later two pink stockings went sliding under the curtain and out onto the cold gray floor.

Nosta's Hike

This is another one of the more personal stories I've submitted, and one I'm especially proud of. This was written in 2018 for a spec-fic anthology on defiance and characters who resist. I probably resisted too far, writing about the isolation of veganism and stepping into areas of nuance, but I stand by the submission, which was presented directly from my own place of defiance and experiences at the time. I hope you enjoy it.

It was hard not to curse after she'd sworn The Path.

And her true feelings about the elves who'd done this, the "heroes" of her glen, well, they lent themselves to cursing.

But cursing was like anything else that harmed. Not the words themselves, of course. But the meaning. It may earn laughs, it may be satisfying, but it wasn't helpful. Declaring elves lesser, broadly deriding their abilities rather than their decisions, or wishing them ill—even masked as advocacy—what would it do?

Nosta was going to be helpful.

Turned out, helpful could be a long, lonely hike.

Her feet ached with the pressure of staying on them all day, and the more horrid feeling of the snow that had melted in through the sides of her boots. The cobbler at the glen only used elk leather. Nosta never had learned to sew more than pillows, so she'd awkwardly made her own boots from canvas scraps—stitching the boot-shapes as best she could, then tacking them to smooth wooden soles, stuffing a small pillow in the bottom of each to cushion her steps.

Ill-fitting and thin, the snow leaked in over time, and her toes swelled, cold and soggy against the cloth.

Coming close to that curse, she trudged on.

The others had never understood her. And if she didn't care for them, things might have been better. But she did. She'd done nothing but care.

They never noticed as she poured her own soaps, made her own meals, and turned down fresh mead, while the others shared. Only when she suggested a small change, something to make a small difference, did they gather and point.

"Why make life more difficult, when we like it so much this way?" they'd ask, irritation in their brows.

Life wasn't about what one enjoyed. It was about what all enjoyed. When would they see that?

They wouldn't like what she was about to do, either. Well, that hadn't stopped her before. She'd started to say she was going out to the mountain. Someone made a joke about gathering herbs, and no one else had bothered to ask. Fine. They'd find out when it was done. She would have answered honestly, too.

The others shook their heads in disbelief when she'd refused the help of the midmen to pull her up the pass. "They could leave if they wanted," the elves said. But they couldn't, not when the elves took all the best land, regulated the rivers, and pointedly rationed the crystals from the mountain.

"They're slaved of your policy, if not your chain," she'd snapped.

"Walk if you want to, then," one had replied. And so she did, without even the benefit of sled tracks to pack the falling snow.

Nosta paused, leaning forward to catch her breath, which clouded before her in a tiny, glittering cloud. A fall of boulders had blocked the way ahead. She considered scaling them—she could climb well enough when she needed to—but the slick face of the rock concerned her.

"Fine," she mumbled, pulling her powders and bowl from her bag.

Nightsbloom was the hardest floral to come by, and she'd hoped not to use any. Most of the glen used wolf's blood for the rupture spell, and they made fun of how weak her nightsbloom concoction was in comparison. Nosta thought that was rubbish; they'd had millennia to perfect the use of wolf's blood, and she'd only been working on this mix for a couple of years. Of course it wasn't as strong. Yet.

She sprinkled the delicate powder into her mixing bowl, adding a pinch of sharpleaf and the smallest amount of ground crystal that she could tap from the tiny vial. Reaching for her flask of lemon oil, she shook in a drop, kneading the resulting paste in her fingers.

"Steady, then," she told herself, pressing her hands and focusing her heart on the rocks ahead.

For a moment, she thought she'd mixed it wrong. Then she felt the sparks in her fingers. First, just a small one, so any animals in the rocks would scurry. Then, when she no longer felt the pull of sentience, she let the rest loose. A fierce crack echoed over the mountain, and she opened her eyes, slowly, hoping she'd done it.

She'd almost done it.

The rock was split, though not fully. Well, she'd make do. Maybe Myria could have fit through, but Nosta was a big elf.

Grumbling, she climbed up into the almost severed rupture, scraping and shimmying her way through until she lowered herself back to the ground.

Dusting the debris from her pants, she continued to climb upward, back and forth as the pass steepened. Around a sharp bend, the screams first reached her.

Loud, furious shrieks. The being hadn't settled in yet; see, she knew they wouldn't. "Keep fighting," she said to the screams in her ears. "I'll help as soon as I can."

It took two more rests before she reached the holding area. Each time, she conjured a tiny heating spell just to warm her feet and dry out her boots and socks. Nosta was used to walking, but not up the height of a mountain. While Nosta stopped, the screeching didn't.

Around the last corner, she saw them—waiting for their "training," as they called it. A brilliant, angry, red dragon.

Chains infused with crystal wrapped their wide neck, each pulling to the side in a large triangle. Screams still filled the air, and all around, the snow had melted and the mud was loose from stomping claws. A spell ward surrounded the hold, creating a thin shimmer in the air.

Seeing Nosta, they lurched forward, grating their rich scales against the harsh metal of the chains. "No, no," she urged, lowering her hands in front of her in calm.

The dragon did not calm.

She sat her bag down again, unable to quell her anxiety, even knowing she was safe outside the ward. Hands now shaking, she pulled her bowl out, searching for anything that might provide her a shield with which to approach.

She couldn't rend the chains. The neck chain was too close

to the being's straining face, and breaking the chains further down would force the dragon to live, indefinitely, wearing an elven collar.

There was no storytale friendship here, either; no quid pro quo for freedom. The dragon reared and kicked, ready to disintegrate any elf in their way. Nosta could understand why. Still, in case it provided any comfort at all, she sang while she worked.

Options ran through her mind, and when she decided which spell might give her the best chance, she worried, for she only had two sprigs of sea nettle left, as its potency only held in the early chill of autumn.

And one almost blew away in the high mountain wind. Smacking her hand against the stem, she exhaled, pulling it close.

Remembering her pledge not to scold herself either, she breathed back in, and focused on creating the mix right the first time. Pausing, she looked down at the second sprig, still poking from the bag. If she used both sprigs, she'd have the best chance, but using both at once meant she wouldn't get a second chance.

"No," she reminded herself, "just not another chance *today*."

She folded in the second sprig and rolled the mixture in her unsteady fingers, willing them steadiness until the paste took its form.

Realizing she hadn't really planned the rest, but not wanting to let the mixture lose potency, she stepped in through the spell ward, freezing as the dragon turned and belched a huge plume of fire in her direction. With a jump, she rolled and tumbled back through the ward, protected from the flames that splattered and crackled in a smooth curve before her.

Her fingers tingling, she hoped she could cast through the barrier. She'd find out. Arms raised upward, she aimed right for the dragon's eyes and cast.

Unwilling to inflict a sleeping spell on the unwitting being that would render them fully helpless, she instead bewildered them, just enough. Or so she hoped. Their eyes went momentarily blank, but it was clear the spell was not fully effective. Yet there was no other batch, and she couldn't let their mistreatment continue.

Barreling through the ward, she pulled herself, using the metal chain, up the dragon's back, grabbing her mother's blade of elven-forged crystal and sawing through the neckpiece until the shackle clattered to the ground.

As the dragon regained coherence, Nosta found herself dangling meters above the ground, barely able to cling to the being's smooth, red neck.

Sliding down their back with more than one bump in the least welcome places, she crumpled into a heap, tripping over her own cloak and landing flat onto her face. She rolled back around.

In that tiny moment between knowing what was coming her way and being able to do anything about it, she saw the split path in front of the dragon. Leave. Or burn Nosta to ashes first.

With a vicious snarl, the dragon bore no mercy in their face. No care. Just a flicker—one small flicker—of understanding what the chilled, bruised elf had done.

Nosta rolled sideways, her fingers digging desperately into

the rock as the percussion from the flapping wings nearly blew her off the side of the mountain.

And then the dragon was gone, a fading red speck in the frost-clouded sky.

Brushing to her feet, she let a long, sing-songy exhale, the sort one permits when others aren't listening. She knew what they'd say when she got back, when she told them what she'd done.

"Not your property to disrupt," they'd shout. Well, not theirs either.

Wanting to be away, she only mixed a small pot of healing and another of warmth, then pulled a mushroom jerky from her pouch, squeezing the savory bites between her chattering teeth.

It would be a long hike down the mountain on her own.

The Irresponsible Enchanter

Back in 2015, Some of my writing contacts were encouraged to try growing an audience through Wattpad. I, while in a break of editing *Shkode*, decided to try it and I published the infamous "Mase the Modern Dwarf" which is goofy and problematic and, I fear, rather dated in tone, and thus I've decided (despite some protests), not to include it here.

There was something interesting about the use of Wattpad in those days. As a non-paying platform (I believe they added ways to pay creators later), there were already various stigmas attached. Yet a couple of my contacts got big attention, drawing massive audiences to their serialized works. The problem: it didn't translate into sales. It's not to say that online serialized fiction can't work this way; I'm attempting it with *Just Bart*, but this wasn't the audience for that transition, so many of us moved along. However, I threw out a couple more pieces, one last one in early 2018, right about the time I went full-time with writing and publishing, and found my time going to other efforts, like establishing a Patreon community.

The other was this, published in mid-2017, with some intent to continue it as a serial.

Even though I stopped using this type of platform, it's important to note that this style of writing—less edited, more free and fun, is one I've tried more and more to embrace, and I think while Mase had his issues, by the time I got to *Just Bart*, I'd gotten that mostly right.

So while I now present to you a Part 1 without a Part 2, I think it's fun, and I hope it stands as an interesting precursor to later serialized efforts.

Content note for non-consensual object enchantment and dark humor.

Part 1: The Other Door

WISTARIA never expected a knock at *that* door.

Wistaria's apartment door opened to a most unremarkable hallway, leading to the long set of stairs she now took every day to work. But it wasn't *that* door. *Tap, tap,* sounded a tiny knock at the closet door she'd enchanted to the other realm. The place she no longer visited. Her old life.

She knew she should have disenchanted the narrow door. But that would require using the magic. Wistaria didn't make magic anymore.

The knocking persisted.

With shaking fingers, she turned the knob. No one was there. She leaned her head against the side of the door.

"We're down here," a small voice said.

Lowering her gaze, she saw a fireplace match and a yellow ball with a drawn-on face, both resting on a red sweater. Her stomach tightened. If this was some sort of prank—

"If you would, Ma'am, we have a request." The voice came from the ball, its marker mouth moving in concert. "You're an enchanter, right?" The sweater's arm released a stone onto the path.

"I was," she answered, her heart sinking. "I'm . . . retired. I live here now." The words, *I don't make magic anymore* on her tongue, she became curious. "Why are you here, anyway?"

"We'd like to be switched back. Just to ourselves again. Also, can you defeat Majestus the Enchanter? He's irresponsible." Ball scowled.

"Irresponsible?" Majestus, yes, she knew him. He had a

reputation for being both powerful and generous. Though, she thought with a glance at her stark apartment, it was a lot easier to be generous when you could conjure gold.

"Yes, he enchants for *sport* and never thinks about the consequences. Like, me, I sit still all day now and don't get played with. The only way I can move is to bounce, and," Ball trembled a small amount.

"It doesn't want to land on its face," Match clarified, an edge to its tone. "And me, I can hop around but, look, I've got one trick, don't I? Then, what, I'm a burnt stick? Forever? I'm a single-use sort. I'd be fine with that. But now—"

Sweater raised its threads to form a simple face, taking care to keep Ball upright as it spoke in a low voice, its arms waggling. "And I'm a sweater. What does an enchanted sweater do that isn't creepy? I mean, I'd strangle Majestus, but he keeps his study locked. Anyway, why'd you quit?"

"MagicList," she murmured, not meaning to say it aloud.

"The website?" Match asked.

"How do you know about a website?" Wistaria didn't mean to sound rude. But she'd never spoken to a match before. And they hadn't seen the reviews.

"It's how we found you. Anyway, could you do it? Switch us back? And battle Majestus?"

"What? I can't battle Majestus."

"Not a wizard battle?"

"Sure, in the middle-ages. Now we have an ethics review board. I could report him, though." The wispy trees of the Realm sparkled outside. She couldn't go back. But, she never liked to turn away someone in need. Yet, disenchanting them—

"If I disenchant you, you won't exist." The three objects

stared at her, their expressions unchanged. Didn't they understand? "That's, you know, *dark*."

"Aren't all enchantment stories dark if you pull the thread far enough? Sorry," Ball added, with a glance to Sweater, whose eyes narrowed a touch.

"Look," Match offered, "if it makes you feel better about it, we just want to be what we were before. I could start a fire. You know, a safe one."

"I could be played with again," Ball said, its marker eyes bright with excitement.

"I could get sweated against without *knowing* about it," Sweater said with a low sigh.

Ball leaned back a touch against Sweater's red yarn, pointing his eyes right up at Wistaria. "You'd be giving us back our purpose."

Wistaria sighed, allowing the tiniest drop of magic to flow into her fingers, ignoring the rush it shot through her body. Yes, a standard enchantment. Easy to reverse. "Well, come in."

Sweater wriggled into the small laundry room, his face expectant.

"Ma'am?" Match said.

"Yes?"

"You promise you'll do it, right? And you'll promise you'll report Majestus? To the, uh, magic ethics board?"

Reporting Majestus would mean reentering the Realm. She glanced through the still-open door, squinting at the beams of light against the shimmering sky. A breeze blew, sending flower petals across the path. "I promise," she answered.

"Then I want to light it." Match hopped down, away from Sweater.

Light it? It doesn't mean—

With a ripping sound, Match lit up in a small blaze. A loud cheer erupted from the others, as Ball teetered and Sweater reached up to steady it. The flame went out, and the char across the top of Match's stick formed into a huge smile.

"You were *awesome*," Ball exclaimed.

"Thanks." Match grinned, its tiny ash smile beaming.

Together, they turned toward her. "We're ready," Ball said.

"Please," whispered Sweater.

With a wave, the three objects dropped to the floor.

Already being in the laundry room, she threw the sweater in her bin, added the burnt match to her compost heap, then looked at the little yellow ball, its marker, now still, forming a perfect smiley-face.

Wistaria tossed the ball into the air and with an easy catch, turned it in her fingers. Walking toward the doorway, she gazed out at the landscape beyond. And stepped through.

Fire Burns Ice

In one of my 2019 attempts to get into a major publication, I figured that I wouldn't have done my job if I passed through this era without one Trumpy story. (And I had forgotten what name I'd used and am cracking up at myself, reading it again.) The response of non-selection took less than 24 hours (*hint hint*), but I appreciated the efficiency. With that, here's my fire mage ditty.

Content note for tyranny and related, non-graphic action.

"SHE'LL come back," Unna rasped. "Keep it burning as long as you can."

She struggled to conceal her own exhaustion, for it would do no good to let them know she could hardly hold the fibers a moment longer. As if hearing her thoughts, the portal wavered, sending a small percussion through her arms. Unna heaved, renewing her grip.

"Look," a boy said, pointing at the impossible sphere weaving through the falling snow. "It wiggled."

"More fuel," his mother urged him, and they ran back into the forest.

Handfuls of brush could not keep this bonfire burning, Unna knew. But it might buy them a few moments longer. And that might be all Mira needed.

"Mage," Heiba called to her, drawing near. They lowered their voice. "Mage, if you don't close it, we'll be out of fuel. We may lose the fire. You must close it."

Unna let her eyelids droop, only accentuating the pain

coursing through her aging fingers. The central fire was their only heat. The villagers relied on it to stay alive.

Mira would return. Mira must return. To Unna's knowledge, only the two of them—Mira and Unna—remained here of the old fire mages, shivering amongst the ice and offering whatever services they could to the outcast villagers.

The ones who had refused to swear to Gahl.

In ages past, anyone could train to be a fire mage; at least, there were no specific limits to it. Barriers of knowledge and access existed, but the mages worked to dismantle them, seeking those who showed the passion. Yet it was nearly impossible here, in the frost of the Outside, to teach the craft. Impossible when they were just trying to survive.

Mira had insisted on going; Unna had offered as well. A second portal would add too much risk, Mira had said. Besides, Unna was older, and life had worn more on her skin. Unna would stand out. Mira's talents thrived on subtlety; she could pass unnoticed.

"I can find it," Mira had contended. "Promise me you'll hold the portal and I'll promise you I'll make it back with the object."

The object was all they called it, for even the villagers didn't know what it was the mages intended to do. Anyone who knew was in danger.

"Please, Mage," Heiba urged. "We can try again another time."

How? How could they try again? Without Mira? Stealth had been critical to getting Inside; any slip would confirm that the portal-maker still lived, would draw Gahl's ire right to where she stood.

She'd tried to explain this to the others; a portal stretched like a rubber band. She'd opened the fibers slowly, but now that they'd had been held, the portal would snap closed with the force of a thunderclap. Mira could shield the effect, but without Mira, their location would be known. Like shooting a flare to Gahl.

If Mira did not return, they'd need to leave. Move on. Hope to survive. Without the element of surprise. Without Mira. Without the object.

"Unna." She heard their voice from her side, closer than before. Urgent. "She's not coming back. We have to call it."

Unna's arms shook. Mira would return with the object. She'd be here. Any moment now. They just needed to—

"She's a mage; she can find a way back."

Maybe. With the right fire and luck. But Mira wasn't a portal-maker and they knew no other way through the boundary. Even if Mira could rend a portal in her desperation, she might emerge elsewhere. She might be alone. Or worse.

"Unna. I'm sorry."

The portal was empty. No shadows emerged at its horizon.

Damn it. Had they really failed? And at the expense of the villagers. Another failure. How long had the villagers gathered the fuel for this now failed attempt? Sacrificed what little they had just to give the mages a chance? The idea stung Unna's heart.

Opening her eyes, she saw Heiba, blurry, beside her. "I'm going to close it."

They slumped in relief.

"Stay with the plan. You must move the village immediately. They will listen to you."

Heiba's eyes widened. "What are you—"

"You said it yourself," Unna hissed. "We had one shot at this. Stealth. Surprise. If supporters find you, tell them I died in the attempt. Burned. You must say I burned. Mira failed. Unna died."

It wasn't even a lie, the way she felt, imagining why Mira might have failed. But there wasn't time for those thoughts. Not yet. "Promise me."

"Mage!"

"Promise."

"I swear to no one," they said, standing taller.

It was the best promise she could get. She smacked her frozen hands together, severing the connection to the dwindling fire. With a howl of pain and nothing but her hip pouch and a weary heart, she hurled herself through the closing sphere.

And tumbled onto the warm ground.

Gahl had even taken away the joy of the warm sunshine on Unna's chapped skin.

She could not allow herself to forget that the sun was only provided to those who pledged to Gahl. Only on the Inside did the fire mages counter the effects of the Chilling. Only to those loyal was fire and warmth made easy.

It would be so easy to stay here.

Her gut wrenched. Hopefully Mira had not decided to stay. Not Mira.

No time to think. She had to move. Looking down at her tattered tunic, she remembered the efforts they'd made to fit Mira with Inside clothes. Thin, clean, and modern, they'd made them from any measure of saved fabric they could find. Family treasures, hewn by dull shears to give Mira a chance of not being recognized.

There was no question which way she should walk. Gahl's gleaming spire towered in the distance, higher than any other structure except the sun itself. With a final wish to dear, strong Heiba for luck and wisdom, Unna set off.

The sweat absorbed into the thick fabric of her tunic as the wetness chaffed her. More than once, she considered the idea of inventing a tale—a way to trade for Inside clothes. Or even to steal them. Yet, with gaunt eyes and thinning limbs, she had the unmistakable look of an Outsider. Supporters, fearful for their own loss of status, would mob her at first sight.

As she walked, she slowly remembered that she was a fire mage, here in a land of heat. If only she could reach a fire before someone noticed her.

She closed her eyes, letting her sixth sense pull her. *Of course.* And so she turned, walking back toward the edge.

The size of the refuse facility was immense. She supposed it needed to be, to process all the discarded items of the entire Inside. Funny, that they wouldn't even let the Outsiders have their refuse. For it was too much risk. Too much risk, with Gahl knowing there could still be two fire mages out there. The two she had not converted.

And that's when Unna saw the projection.

Gahl did not wear ceremonial robes or dark attire. She

dressed as many Insiders might: casual and unconcerned. But when her image was projected out into the center of the intake lot, she was ten times her own height.

"Greetings," she waved. "You will be so pleased with the news that I have for you today. Thanks to me, there is one less traitor on the loose, as Mira, one of the last two unholy practitioners, has recognized my greatness—our greatness—" she added with a smirk, "and arrived at the Gahl Center for conversion. You are all now safe from her, because of me. She is behind closed doors with no access to fire."

Gahl continued on with the standard projection, praising the people for their devotion and letting them know all the things she was improving. Even as Unna's heart dropped, she had to remind herself: Gahl was not a mage. Gahl lied for her own benefit.

Unna would not give up on Mira.

And it was with extra passion that Unna drew in the flames from the incinerator's plume, ignoring the shouts and calls of those who saw the aberration. With a burst, Unna shot into the air and darted inward, right toward the gleaming upper discs of the Center.

With a gasp, she landed on an outdoor patio, her bare hands almost burning at the heat of the sun against its planks. She rolled over, groaning, as the last of the magic fled her. The flight, a basic skill, had made her feel like a broken pane of glass. Deprived of the magic for so long, it now ached in her every bone.

Determined, she forced herself to stand, heaving her breath in and out again. She didn't have to cast. She just had to find the object. No, and Mira too. Find the object, which they knew Gahl must keep close by. Then find Mira. Then get out.

Struggling now just to move her aching limbs, Unna stumbled toward the patio windows. Supporters milled down the hallway, not seeing her through the tinted glass that shielded them from the bright sun. These would be the most loyal supporters, to be allowed on the upper levels. No, not the most loyal, she corrected. The most powerful. The most loyal were living out there in the warm air, either not believing or not caring about the stories of the frozen lands beyond their view.

Powerful supporters—who made the choice to be both, rather than risk the former. What would happen when one of them turned? Or two?

The one thing Unna had kept from freezing all these years was her heart. And she would not give up that others had one too. She would never give up. That was why the object was critical. Unna took a breath.

If she was going to search Gahl's rooms without being stopped, she needed two things: appropriate clothing, and a whole lot of luck. Waiting for a break in the wandering supporters, she slid the door open and stepped inside. This disk featured living quarters; she needed to find an unoccupied room.

Carefully, she held her ear against each door. The fourth door sounded silent. She took one of the fragments from her pack, and removed her hidden flint. There was just enough fire in the little piece of fuel to allow her to cast an opening spell.

Concentrating, she raised her arm to strike the flint, and a hand grabbed her opposite wrist. The little chunk of fuel thunked onto the floor. *No!*

A man grabbed her raised arm, pulling it downward and behind her. There was no question how they would have found her so quickly. She almost closed her eyes, but it would do no good. Across from her stood Mira.

She'd hoped for a clear sign in Mira's eyes. Either the spark of defiance: the secret signal that she was faking her compliance. Or a clear sign of betrayal, the weight of a lifetime colleague who had lied about the whole plan.

There was neither. Mira looked scared. She opened her mouth, perhaps with an explanation of what she had done. Or why. Instead, she closed it.

Unna looked away as they were led down the hallway.

"Don't let her have fire," Gahl barked from a large, circular room. "Search her; take everything." Around the sides were lofty cages, surrounded by bars. Unna reeled in disgust. Was Gahl so paranoid she kept holding cells by her own chambers?

"Is this all you have?" Gahl said, pointing at the small chunk of fuel. She laughed.

Unna stared at the cages; they had the luxury of being warm and clean. More than the villagers had. This sickened her as her small pack was untied and her pockets patted down. She thought how long the villagers had searched for those few nuggets of fuel that Gahl now mocked.

"Check again. Check her hands, her pockets. There can be nothing."

Unna did not hide her disgust as the guards' uncaring hands rummaged around her body. Even with the horrors of the Outside, no one touched her this way. "Is this how you are taught to touch the elderly here? Is this what you follow?"

Gahl snorted, turning to her guards. "If she had her way, we'd be overrun. Think of how the elderly would be touched then."

Yet, Gahl quickly had the mages pushed into two separate cells, and only after the locks clanged shut did she dismiss the guards. "I'm sure you'll want to catch up," she added with a grin. "You have no power here, as you'll quickly learn. I'll be back later. When I get to it." She laughed, stomping from the room.

They sat in silence for a long while. Unna had so many questions, but she knew, of course, that Gahl would be listening. Probably Gahl herself, without knowing what conversations they might have.

"It's different here," Mira finally said. "Different than we describe it. The warmth—" Her voice cracked and she glanced away.

Unna understood. Being a fire mage, so long separated from everything she'd studied and refined, and to suddenly be free from the constant chill in her bones— What Unna didn't know is whether Mira was turning, or whether she wanted Gahl to think so. Unna couldn't ask her.

"You know the sacrifice it took to send you here." It was all she could think to say. "No amount of projections will make me forget that."

They sat a while longer. "We were the last two," Unna said. Of the old group, she didn't add. Sometime, someday, another would learn. They would find a way. Unna believed that. "Our legacy will be that we left them. And never returned."

Pain clouded Mira's face. Unna stopped. If Gahl was here to force ideas on Mira, Unna was not. She exhaled. "I'm sorry. You know the situation."

Again, they sat in silence. The silence was unlike Mira, but then again, so was running away.

"I knew you would come," Mira whispered. "I'm sorry. They've taken everything from me. I've . . . pledged to Gahl."

Sickness wrenched her gut, squeezing the hunger and exhaustion that were already there. "Then why are you still here?" Unna couldn't help but ask. She pointed at the bars.

"It takes time. To earn trust. Just like it took time when we first met, when you first left me the note at my bedside."

Unna forced an audible giggle as her mind spun. It was as though Mira was suggesting they'd been lovers. They hadn't. They'd really barely been friends, pushed together by the circumstance of the Chilling.

Then, she understood. Calming, she wondered how long it would take. Better if Gahl was truly alone, spying on the mages, yet not surrounded by her cleverer sycophants. Mira rambled on. A picnic they'd taken. How much she missed the warmth, and how good it was to feel it again.

There was nothing in this cell that she could use. Sparse, careful, they'd made no mistakes.

Not true. They'd made one.

With a flick of her wrist, Unna slid the tiny flint from her sleeve. Throwing all her clothes over her head and past her ankles as fast as she could, she snapped the little device.

Come on!

Snap . . . snap.

A spark lit. The clothing, crusty with dried sweat, burst into flames and Unna wasted no time. Drawing in every flame, she bent the cage bars, bent Mira's cage bars, then flew, naked, through the corridors, blinking ahead in patches, looking for any sign of Gahl's bedroom.

Her chamber was unmistakable, with billowing drapes and

piles of silken pillows. A bed that could fit ten. And a small table to its side. She wrenched open the drawer and grasped the object into her left hand, pulling it upward. The strength of the enchantment nearly overwhelmed her, yet she kept a firm grip.

Desperately clicking the little flint, she lit the bed. She lit the pillows. She lit the drapes. Even a hint of magic allowed her to fan the sparks, bursting them into flames. And her sweating, naked body took in every element of the burning heat, warming it, filling it.

"Stop her! Do whatever you need!" Gahl shouted, hoarse, stumbling in the smoke of the doorway.

Sweeping every flame available into her spirit, for this would take everything she had, Unna concentrated on the idea of Outside—not a specific place, but the idea, so that they would not know where to find her—and wrenched her arms open, prying the burning blue sphere.

Mira. Where is Mira?

Gahl's supporters flooded into the room and in the flash she had to decide, she thought of the Outside. And stepped through, smacking the portal closed with every spark she had left.

Freezing now, her skin turned almost immediately to ice as she slid across a frozen lake, her fist held tightly against her. Slowly, she reached forward, finding something to grasp with her free hand, but found nothing. She tried to stand, but slid, slamming her chin onto the ice.

Mira. Maybe Mira got out. Mira would be the last of the old mages. *Mira.*

She would not give up, but without relief from the long, smooth ice, she could not rise or even pull herself along. Her mind clouded and muscles screamed, hoping someone would hear.

"Over there. I told you." It was a small voice, a young girl, perhaps. Unna closed her eyes.

Unna woke up to an ill-fitting gown and a cocoon of scratchy blankets. She couldn't imagine who was going without for one stranger to have so many blankets. Her eyes focused to a room of people huddled in a rock-walled shelter.

"Are you really her? The mage?" A woman her own age stared back, with narrow eyes peeking out from behind a tightly-wrapped scarf. The light of a small lamp flickered over her face.

Unna nodded. "Yes." But she couldn't quite remember—where had she gone? She gasped. "Gahl will look for me! You are not safe with me here. Thank you; you saved my life. But I must go." She tried to sit up, though it was difficult under all the blankets.

"What's this?" The little girl held out an object: a small cube painted with a single eye, radiating lines of gilded light. Unna stared. How could she have forgotten?

"It's Gahl's projector. I took it."

No one spoke. No one needed to.

"You took it to stop the projections?"

"More than that," Unna answered, the pieces fluttering back into her mind. "She will find another way to communicate. Her lies cannot be our focus. Only the truth can be. We took the object"—she thought with pain of Mira—"to show people the truth. The Outside."

The woman stood up, rising into a towering figure against the wall of the small room. "We must use it right away. As you say, she will be looking. We have this chance; we must take it."

"Please, let me go first. It is too dangerous, and she will know where it projected from the moment that it's used." *Or at least . . . any mages will that are supporters*, she thought with sadness.

"What will you project? The forest? It is us she attacks; show them us."

With a deep breath, Unna nodded.

"Here," the woman held out a small object: her flint. Grateful, Mira took it into her scraped fingers. She loosened the blankets and rose into a seat.

The little girl handed her the object and Unna reached it over the fire, allowing the wood to warm. It didn't need much; the enchantment was tremendous. The eye opened, and Unna turned it around the room. She wondered if Mira was watching.

"This is the Outside. These are the people who have questioned Gahl and refused to pledge. We live here, freezing, devoid of comfort or even moments of peace or true rest. Families. Friends. They have given me three blankets because I had a chill, while they huddle, shivering, around me. This is the Outside. Why do we oppose her? Because we are *free*. We will live under no monarch. We will not accept comfort so others may suffer. We—"

The device sputtered out, and Unna screamed, dropping it. "Severed," she sputtered, catching her breath. "Such power. More than we have here. Endless fire." She glanced at the burns on her hand, quickly turning her palms inward so the others wouldn't see.

"They will come here?" the older woman asked.

"Yes," Unna whispered. "You must go."

Unna spun around trying to see where the projector had landed, and instead she saw a pair of hands, covered in torn gloves, clasping the object.

"I will find you," he said, running from the cave.

The woman began to cry, a stifled cry without the means for tears. "We will be slow, with the children. He knows now that we cannot say where it is."

To the side, the little girl began to howl. "Grampa!"

Taking it all in, Unna sat a long moment, hearing only the child's cry and the woman's stifled sniffles. Slowly, others began to murmur, in somber, muted tones.

She imagined what the projection might have looked like, a cave of two dozen huddled people, of icy walls and a tiny, muted flame.

The other mages. They had seen.

This was no victory; not yet. It was just another moment. And they must brace, now, for the arrival of Gahl's supporters. They would search, and Gahl would not relent until she had discredited the rumors, until her humiliation had faded. She would send the supporters after them. The other mages, those who had pledged to Gahl. Sadly, Unna did not know what lengths they would go to, how cold the warmth had made them.

Unna would not join them. Truth would always fight. And as long as these people thought for themselves, there was hope. As long as the fire burned somewhere, then it still burned.

"You must go," she said to the woman.

She looked about to speak, but then did not. Their eyes met.

Shedding the blankets and with only the thin gown around her, Unna ran off, into the night.

Virus

I wrote this 11 March 2020, in bed, after President Trump's prime-time COVID-19 address.

TRUMP-16 causes unkindness and separation.
  Cures are available.

Offbeat Tattoo

This is one I am really proud of. It was for a collection of alternative Beatles stories in 2019. I was going to write a story about Wizard Beatles, but when I saw that theme was being used already by an invited author and you could only submit one piece, this one came to mind. I really hope you will enjoy it.

Ringo looked up from the front desk as the string of copper bells jangled against the door. A woman walked in, lanky and projecting an air of unease. Ringo pushed her brown curls away from her eyes. "Can I help you?"

"Yeah, I'd like a tattoo. Something we can do now, if possible."

Ringo reached under the counter and pulled out three dogeared binders. "Artists' portfolios—you'll want to get a sense of which style you prefer. Was just going on a smoke break. G won't let me smoke inside," she explained. "But maybe someone can cover while you're deciding." She reached back and drew over the thick curtain separating the desk from the back room.

A cozy parlor came into view, with chrome padded benches and walls striped in colorful flash.

"That's the cop," Jo said, setting down a sketchbook and wandering up toward the desk. A mix of gray tattoos melded with her dark skin, winding out from under her cropped canvas jacket and white tee. Thin locs were pulled back with an army-green scarf, framing a pair of small, round glasses. "The Sergeant, right?"

The woman rested her hand on the sketchbook. "I should go," she muttered.

"Nah, no need," Jo said. "We serve love, humor, and tattoos. Looks like you could use a little of each? Now, what was it? Bully boss? Bad acid?"

The Sergeant's head shot up.

"Oh, just a joke. Got a record, you know." Jo didn't quite look like she was joking.

"Yeah. I try, but the brass have a thing about other people's business." She sighed. "Call me Lydia. And it's a break up. Bad one. Don't really want to talk about it."

"Mic, did you hear that? We got a lonely heart."

Another woman approached, short, stout, and wearing a plain black shirt. Chunky tattoos ran down her arms, their bold colors picking up the yellows in her tousled hair. "My advice?" Mic leaned in. "Don't get a sad tattoo. Get a happy one."

The buzzing of a tattoo machine stopped in the background. "Well, she ought to get the one she wants," G said, joining them, her fringed tunic swaying as she moved. "New machine," she said, pointing back to a side table. "Was getting the feel of it." She reached out, her fingers covered in a variety of symbols. Lydia shook the offered hand, looking up at the woman, who was half a head taller even than the solidly-built cop.

"Hi. Lydia? Call me G. Short for Georgie. Works for T.G. too." She winked, letting go. "These three will go on all day at you, but what we want is for you to get what suits you best. If you're looking for art, Jo'll get you, but she'll do it her way, so be warned. Mic draws clean and bright; you'll love whatever she comes up with."

"What about you?" Lydia asked.

"She can do anything," Ringo interrupted. "And me, I ink also. Just did a trippy octopus design if you'd like to see it."

Jo snorted as Mic shook her head.

"Oh, be nice," G said. "Wouldn't be our shop without Ringo here, and they know it. So, what you looking for?"

Lydia seemed like she was about to answer, but her face drew with emotion. She turned away.

"You know what this needs?" Jo said, giving a nod to Ringo. Ringo smiled, and pulled two pencils from a battered metal cup. She started to tap on the desk in a precise rhythm, as Jo closed her eyes and hummed a few long notes. G grabbed a rubber band from her table and stretched it over her fingers, plucking with the other hand to create a simple bassline.

> *It's just an ordinary day,* Jo sang.
> *Whatever other people say*
> *Your lonely heart is in good company*
> *Here . . . with my friends and me*

Jo switched to humming a harmony as she nodded to Mic, who took over the melody.

> *Friends will pull you through*
> *No matter what you're going through*
> *And if your day doesn't feel the way you hoped it to*
> *Stop on by; we'll all join in a song or two*

With a nod from Mic, all four sang together, in harmony:

> *Friends will pull you through*
> *No matter what you're going through*
> *Take that lonely heart and let it fill with love*
> *Bask in the sunshine of the friends who care for you*

Then they stopped, G releasing the rubber band and Ringo setting her pencils down on the desk. Jo and Mic bumped arms, while cutting each other an amused glance.

Lydia laughed, a mirthful laugh laced with excised pain. "Thanks. I can't thank you enough." She exhaled, her breath shaking a touch. "That's just what I needed."

"Free of charge," Jo quipped. "We're simply happy to help."

"I'd still like a tattoo," she said, patting the binders. "If you're willing."

"Of course," G said. "It's why we're here."

"Would it be strange if we drew a heart—" She traced the shape on her arm. "—and each of you added to it? I think that would be perfect."

"We'll do our best," Mic said.

Ringo grinned. "Just need to see your ID, and need you to sign this." She pulled a notepad from the shelf, sliding a piece of cardboard under the first set of carbons. "Last name?"

"Pepper," she answered. Relaxing a touch, she scanned the room. "And thanks again."

Wednesday's Robes

So I mentioned that my first thought for the anthology of alternative Beatles stories was Wizard Beatles. Thinking of this, my mind went right to a specific moment in the Beatles' career, and right to the idea of what it might look like visualized as Wizard Beatles, navigating a land of gray robes and grayer expectations. When I realized that a wizard piece was being written by one of the invited authors, I thought submitting another wizard piece, even if different, was too much of a risk. But, feeling the pull of it, I wrote my little wizard moment anyway. It never was really polished since I shifted back to the submitted piece, but as a snapshot into my original vision, I thought you would enjoy it.

"They'll never let us in like this," Palomacannthry worried, running his hands over the thick fabric. From above, the gold light of the huge, vaulted window cast a rather holy glow over the new ensemble.

"Are we wizards or are we not?" Jolennion asked. "I'm tired of casting bit spells for their validation when we're capable of so much more."

Just then, Georthrarissn swept into the hall, securing a large velvet cap over her tight brown curls. "I agree. Wizarding won't *grow* if we let them bump us down the same wagon trail. Besides, who's drawing the crowds? If they like that look so much, *they* can get out there and rally the villagers. If it's up to us, we do it our way. Now, are you ready?"

As the men nodded, Georthrarissn walked to an old brass

handle, swinging open a huge pair of doors, which opened to a bright sky overlooking the mountains. "Ringo!" she called. "We're ready if you are!"

They stood, watching, as a large pink dragon swept down from the middle of a cloud and into the center of the circular room. He let a small friendly roar.

"Ringo!" Jolennion warned, as they all dodged the sparks of fire coming from the dragon's broad snout. Giving the wizard a gentle nudge back, Ringo lowered himself down, allowing the others to climb onto his back.

Together, they flew off toward the elven forest.

When the wizards of the B'Tles conclave arrived in the midst of the gathering of magic, the collective gasp of those gathered was certainly heard around the world.

Stunned, a sea of pointed caps and properly-fitted gray robes stood like statues as each of the arriving wizards slid down Ringo's back and onto the raised tree stump of old Mother Tree, A'lalna'tran'qwia.

In contrast to Ringo's bright pink scales, Jolennion wore robes of brightest yellow. Fringe, cords, buttons, and a smattering of glitter covered his robes, and instead of a wizard cap, he simply wore a small set of round glasses.

Beside him, Palomacannthry was dressed in a blue brighter than the most dazzling elven sky, even more decorated than Jolennion, and holding a mage's scepter of obscene length.

Eclipsing them, Georthrarissn slid to the ground, in huge robes of orange, lace, and corded glamor, and with a massive tricorne hat, whose orange sheen and woven gold trim glimmered in the sunlight. "Meet the B'Tles," she said, her voice projecting out over the crowd.

Behind her, Ringo reared up on his hind legs, breathing a steady plume of fire.

Wizard wands and elven banners rose into the air in protest, as a chorus of shouts arose.

"This is not how wizards dress!"

"Our values are defunct!"

"They must leave!"

Jolennion turned to the others, a huge grin across his face. "Actually, why are we here? We don't need crowds of gawking mages. Not when we have the villagers."

Georthrarissn grinned. "Sounds right to me. Let's get out of here." Louder, to the crowd. "I apologize—but it's time for us to go."

"Let's go make some magic," Palomacannthry agreed.

Singing loudly together in perfect harmonies, the B'Tles piled onto Ringo's back and flew off into the sunshine, a mass of colorful fringe billowing in their wake.

Breath and Harm

My first attempt to get into a publication I greatly respect was turned down with some nice compliments (I was thrilled), but saying that the stakes were not high enough. (You will read this one, "Rain's Cloud", near the end of this collection.)

So when I tried again in 2019, I tried to imagine what stakes could be very high, without traditional violence. And this is what I came up with.

I was worried about submitting it, and told the editor so. I was worried in a super tense political environment, people would read into it things I did not mean. The story is more of a subtle frustration, and less of a directed message, than people might make it. (I am less worried about any misinterpretation of the nuance here, where you know me, but I was nervous to submit this into a broader view.)

The editor really liked the piece; I was very honored. And the themes did not bother him—but he wished some of the elements were tied back in more tightly. He is renowned and I value his opinion greatly, but that *is* my style and I know not everyone likes it. He said he might consider a shorter version focusing on one of the scenes. I was welcome to resubmit.

But I didn't. I would be open to editorial feedback on this story, but cutting it felt like a different story. Again, he might be right by most standards. But I like this version, and I decided to preserve it, for you to enjoy here.

I hope that you do. (And I do hope to get into this publication someday. I will try again.)

Not every magia chose to be a warrior. But, Tresa thought in that moment when all breath ceased, perhaps if she had been one, she could have done something to stop it.

Yet if Tresa had been a warrior, her breath would have stopped as well.

It was a fluke that she'd escaped the cursed wind. Every evening, as she had for decades, Tresa had been sitting, cross-legged under her vine-hatched window, practicing her sequence. Trying to calm her mind.

The sequence of protection looked like nothing to an observer. Unlike the sequence of the huntress, the sequence of the swordwielder, or the sequence of the swan, there were no sweeping forms or loud incantations. The sequence of protection flowed through portals of understanding: it traversed the worlds of here and there and felt the space between. It wove through the complexity of elation and energy. And to an observer, it looked only like an old woman, seated under a window.

Tresa had been on the third form, in the plasma between freedoms, when the wind had blown through. And when she emerged from the seventh form, not refreshed but prepared for another day, she felt the change.

"Marn?"

The young boy cleaned the windows and rafters, for Tresa could no longer reach them with her creaky back and precarious wrists. Standing, Tresa pulled on her shawl and walked, slowly, into the next room. Terror doubled within her—not just the terror in the air, but the terror of uncertainty for what the first feeling could mean.

Marn rose on one tiptoe, reaching over an awkwardly jutting ledge. His other leg stuck out behind him, and a rag dangled between his fingers and the shelf.

He was a statue. Alive in memory only.

Tresa circled him, one side to the other, wondering who could do such a thing. And what was this curse—would his body teeter here, dusting her ledge for eternity? Would he decay? What if the supports under him were removed; would he fall? Hesitantly, she touched his extended arm. The boy was immovable. She stood on a chair to view his face. It held no fear, no concern. Only mild irritation for the height and the dust.

He never knew.

While she didn't want the boy to suffer, this detail felt macabre in its own right, bothering her more than she expected. Everyone should have the right to face their own death. Not have it whisked from them, without even a goodbye.

For there was no question this had been done intentionally. Who? Who would do this?

Clearly a magia. Perhaps registered, perhaps not. But someone trained in flower dust and platinum sparks. Someone with a key.

She was ready to burst through the draperies of the sanctum itself, demanding answers. Yet a protection magia understood caution. The fire burned in her mind. The light glowed in her fingers.

First, to discover the extent of the violation.

Tresa took a walking stick and her most comfortable satchel, and she set out for the village. She walked, step by step and using no magic, for she could not take the risk of exposing herself yet.

Maybe this was all just an attack on Marn. She knew that

it was not. No one would harm little Marn, not specifically. For anyone who would do such a thing would not see him as important. And on that, they would be wrong twice.

She ambled toward the village, keeping to the shadows. At the first sight of the figures, the tears fell unhindered from her eyes. They streamed down her face. There was nothing to investigate; the signs sprawled in front like graffiti on a shrine.

Two young children played in a field, outside the village. One was young, wearing a ruffled dress with torn stockings and worn shoes—stopped halfway through rolling down a hill. And the second was likely a sibling, an annoyed look on their face. Probably tasked to watch the younger child with no notion the excursion would be their last.

She walked further into the village. An older woman, perhaps her age, heaved on the rope from the well. No one had offered to help her, or perhaps she had refused, but the water was needed and now she froze in its labor.

Behind a tree, two young women hid. Their expressions mixed in fear, trepidation, and joy, as they held each other close. As a statue, it would have brought her glee. As a fracture of life, it sickened her, and brought acid to her throat. "I will help," she whispered, averting her eyes from the secreted lovers.

Street after street, her pain deepened. A man steadied his back from the ache of tilling a vegetable garden. A family dipped in the stream, their arms raised in a splash that had long since flowed away. A youth sat on a bench, looking like they had something to decide. A child glanced behind a shed. Even a squirrel curled around a branch, tail puffing behind.

There was no life left in the world.

Tresa walked toward the sanctum.

At first, she resisted the powder, for it would do no good to be detected. But her rage overtook her—her frustration—and she drew the pouch from a pocket. So little was left; no one respected the protection magia and though they were given polite words and righteous nods, no one hired them for tasks. Perhaps she should save the pinch that she had, but she wanted to fly.

Injustice tried her patience.

Tresa grasped the wind, twisted it, and flew toward the sanctum, allowing the rush of the wind to fill her. She did not reject its high; she consumed it, hoping it would speed her way.

The sanctum loomed ahead, its three towers glinting in the sun's bright light. Did the magia know what had happened? The rest of them, she meant, other than the magia that had stopped the breath.

She slowed her approach, landing on her toes behind a glistening silverthread tree. On the path ahead stood a magia, as immobile as the people of the village.

Tresa was out of tears. Glancing about, she tiptoed toward the path. She recognized this one, though their name escaped her. Tall and handsome, they had a smile on their face as though enjoying the slow warmth of the morning sun. Only a hint, just a flicker, traced their eyes, as though they'd felt the wind, perhaps only in the moment that it hit them.

Her hand hovered over the magia's arm, yet she did not touch them. She had nothing to offer; a protection mage could only offer a depth of insight. They could offer the tools to heal, but not the healing itself. That had to come from within.

Or in this case, it could only come from the magia who

had done this. That magia, Tresa must find. All life depended on it.

She did not diminish caution as she slipped around the edges of the courtyard. She did not move toward the figures gathered around, each one illuminated clearly in the streams of midday light. Talking, studying, or practicing forms, they held steady within a moment.

Tresa's heart ached at what they might have done differently if they knew that moment would be their last. She exhaled, determined it could not be.

There was a thread of hope. If only one magia remained, they would be easy to sense. This was also a thread of despair, because Tresa would be just as easy to find. Only slightly less, for she was not glowing with the amount of dust this wind would have required.

This meant two things. One, Tresa must move quickly, before that imbalance restored. Two, the magia was not here, because if they were, Tresa would have already lost.

She looked at the flower dust in her hands. Powder, only. And, so, whispering apologies into the spaces of protection, she moved quickly through the corridors, searching pockets and bags for each magia's supply.

With just enough in her satchel, she sped away again. The trail was not difficult, nor the logic, once she considered it. Wafts of power flowed from the mountains, where the winds blew in constant gales, and any such force would have been amplified by the carvings of nature.

She shivered at the cold, for her shawl was nothing against the gusts of snowy air. Sparing a touch more of the powder, she cast a layer of warmth, preventing her from shivering as she approached the lone magia. Then another, larger, pinch to shield herself.

"Who is here?" Tresa called.

A form spun out from behind a boulder and Tresa reeled at the force of the wind against her. The ice crystals gave it an almost corporeal form, and she watched as each strand bent and shattered around her shield.

Without enough powder to sustain the shield—or her heat—for long, she'd have to talk quickly.

She knew this magia. Jiloe. Tresa stumbled, and almost dropped her shield. Gasping, she reformed it just as Jiloe threw another wind past.

Jiloe was no villain. Jiloe was a hero. No magia had fought harder for the treatment of people, animals, and the land itself. She spoke when the others turned away. She was a warrior of ice with a heart of flame.

"Why?" Tresa's voice trembled. She noticed Jiloe's eyes were red; her hair unkempt.

"They harm, and harm, and they won't stop. They harm themselves. Each other." She stopped, her attention flighty. "Let me freeze you. I have enough. It will save you from the pain."

"No," Tresa whispered. "The pain is life, Jiloe. You know that."

"I know? Do you know what I know? Fight the harm, they begged me. You're not doing enough, they shouted. Not enough to stop the ones that interfere in others' lives; lives they know nothing about. For ignorance. For greed. It doesn't matter; they harm and harm and won't stop. So I tried to find a form, a way to mark the harmful. Some were easy, their actions plain in sight, and so I continued on, not wanting to miss anyone."

Tresa wished she could ease her shield, for the pain in her shoulders and her waning hand of powder, but she dared not. She stayed quiet, listening to Jiloe.

"*This one. That one.* They pointed. *He is wrong. She is lost.* And I tried to mark their hearts, and I felt the pressure of ill ideas, the way others suffered for their flaws or their greed. Then I moved to the next, the ones claiming goodness. But there were fibers between them. For many, their elders were among the marked. What would it do to sever those webs, when their upbringing had made them the people that they were, working to change the minds of others? What would it do to them now? I marked them also."

Jiloe's breath intensified. "And the essence of one that I had marked struck me, and I saw the rigor of his charity. It did not negate the harm but it left me confused. And in my confusion one of the good touched me as well; their pettiness and rancor burned me like a searing needle and I wondered what harm was spread among the so-called good. And so I marked more.

"And one who was marked had clouds of such darkness that the others could not comprehend. And one who spoke words of righteousness acted not in their stead. Then one pointed to the other and the same pointed back, and their arguments were each flawed. I marked more, and more, and more. And only the good were left, but their words, their sadness, they overwhelmed me, and the insects crushed under their stomping feet, and I understood: all who breathe harm. Some more than others, but all in their ways. I could judge the acts and ideas for myself but I could not sever the fabric of beings who contained them.

"I will show you!" Jiloe stopped suddenly, and surrounded by vines of color, she whisked into the air and away from the site.

Tresa followed, wrapping herself in a thin layer of warning only, enough to sense any ill-intent. And they landed, in a town square, packed with people. Jiloe pointed and spun, her reddened eyes blazing. "Look!"

Right before her, a pair locked in place. One's fist had been cocked back, ready to strike. And the other howled, with words now lost. A child cried. Around them, arms were raised, and mouths extended, and faces pinched in fury. "Look at them!" Jiloe implored.

"You are not a god!" Tresa shouted, letting her protection drop and channeling her remaining powder into the strength of her words alone. "You do not decide who stands and who falls. Each of us—we control our power. We control our choices. We do not control each other! Jiloe, you fight the acts, not the people. You fight the harm, not the world."

Jiloe leaned against the person with the raised fist, and sobbed into their tunic. "It hurts!" She raised her head.

"I know," Tresa whispered. "This is not the way."

"Why not? If it ends the pain?"

"It does not end the pain," she said. "Harm is not breath. Harm is control. Exerting control to end the harm makes more control. It spins the tornado; it does not calm it."

"It can't be so simple," Jiloe finally said.

"It's not," she replied.

They stood together, a very long time. The shadows under the posed villagers shifted in slow contrast to their still forms, but Tresa dared not move until Jiloe's tears were through.

"I can't undo it," Jiloe said. "The dust that I used—it was a lifetime collected."

Tresa knew. It would have to have been. "We will gather it from the sanctum. Together. Come, I will not leave you."

"Steal their powder?" Jiloe stepped back.

"How can they use it now?"

She nodded, seeming unable to speak.

As they flew back together, Tresa not revealing she was flying only on the dust of powder left in her hands, she considered that she would be defenseless now if Jiloe changed her mind. Tresa would stay here, frozen in mid-air, for as long of an eternity as Jiloe wished.

Terrified, she wondered if Jiloe could freeze herself.

And so she kept very still, very quiet, as they canvassed the towers, searching pockets and desks and satchels for one vessel of dust after another.

The evening light was golden when Jiloe said they had enough. Instead of the mountain, she flew back to an open hill, basking in the warming light. "The magia will have no power for a while, if I do this," she finally said.

Tresa knew she was referring to the powder they had taken, as much as they could find. It would take years to gather a new supply. Anything that remained would be donated for essential functions only, including to run the platinum forge. Yes, she should have considered that before she acted, Tresa thought but did not say.

"No, Jiloe," she said instead. "We will still have our voices. Our examples. Our spirits. Our hands." She held out her wrinkled palms, but Jiloe gazed outward, over the hill.

As Jiloe glowed gold and extended her arms in a form of the

warrior, Tresa felt overwhelmed by the heat of the incantation, and she flew, with the small powder she had kept, back to the town square. The one Jiloe had shown her.

Tresa watched, as a wave of light seared across the sky and the raised fist bolted forward, knocking into the other's jaw as blood spattered out in an arc. The child screamed, and the people shouted in glee.

And Tresa collapsed back onto a low stone wall, unsure what she had done.

Rachel

So this is a strange one, and does have a violent content note, so it's one many of you will want to skip. But I think some of you may appreciate this different angle to my writing and perspective, so I decided to include it.

This story was originally written in 2016 for a horror collection centered around a fictional town with pre-set worldbuilding that included a haunted tree, specific characters, and tales of missing children. I did it because (in addition to me still feeling things out back then) one of the editors was (is) a friend and they were going to sell the book, with donated stories, for charity.

And I had another motivation, one that grabbed me at the time. When I thought of horror, I immediately considered fully expressing myself as a vegan. Vegan horror, aka political satire. So I did.

My friend's press closed down before publishing the book, and another press picked up the title. I was fine with my story being included—I mean, it was a very specific story. However, realizing that the book turned out as *comedic* horror involving children (an unappealing combination to many) and never having any contact with the press anyway, it's not a book I'm promoting. As for my little statement, to date, not a single person has ever remarked on this story to me, in person, in a review, anywhere.

I hope that those willing to read the piece will see it for what it is, and I worked pretty hard on juxtaposing my political satire over pretty prose for extra effect. That said, I will not write this type of story again.

Content note for gory violence and death. It's fine to skip this one. (Or maybe it'll turn you vegan?)

THE sun always sets early in the valley.

Edwin hustled down the dimming street, clutching a parcel in his rough, chapped fingers. He stared at the ground, hoping no one would notice him. It was Sunday night, and he was running late.

The street ended just ahead, and Edwin grimaced at the men standing on the walkway to either side. Mr. Harper paced outside the Town Hall, doing whatever the strange man did outside the Town Hall every night, alone. And across the street Mayor Graves leaned against a post, talking to the Constable.

Edwin grunted. There was no way to avoid them both. He glanced a moment at the Mayor, who stood pinching a monocle in his left eye and twisting a lavish scarf Edwin was certain to be intended for a woman. And the Constable—he avoided him at all costs. The man would ask about Rachel. Always, about Rachel. About how she'd gone, and where she was.

Edwin knew where Rachel was.

And he'd never tell them. They wouldn't understand; maybe they'd even send him away. No, he'd never leave this place.

Even if he hated it.

Mr. Harper it was, then. Edwin veered to the left. "Well, hallo, Edwin, it's almost Monday, isn't it?" Mr. Harper said in a sing-song voice, as he tipped his wide-brimmed hat over his broadening grin.

Edwin grunted, with a slight nod he hoped would pass for a greeting.

"I'll be by, you know. Early, too. Spring lamb is our favorite; we wouldn't miss the loin for anything. Be sure and cut it for chops!"

"I always do," Edwin muttered, his eyes planted ahead.

The road thinned as he entered the trees, and his cabin slipped into view.

Too dark, he thought. *Will need to hurry.*

He scraped his boots on the coarse mat and listened for the sound of the rocking chair. Back and forth, it creaked. Like a heartbeat. The only heartbeat that was left of the two women he loved.

It was enough. It had to be.

The chair continued its lullaby as he approached. "Beloved," he whispered, leaning in to give his wife a kiss. The blanket had slipped a bit; he tucked it back around her shoulders. "I'm sorry, but I've got to hurry if I'm going to see her. There's clouds tonight."

He didn't expect her to respond, her blank eyes fixed on the worn quilt which covered the window before her. He turned to leave.

"She needs friends."

Edwin rested his hand in a gentle caress against her drooping chin. "I'll take care of her, Ilana. Always." Ilana gave no answer, except for the rhythmic rocking of the chair.

It was cold in the shed, but there was no time to build a fire. He'd have to make do. The rifle leaned against the stove. He swept a bullet from the tool chest, and dropped it into his pocket.

The lamb was waiting, outside, tied to a post. It kicked against the dirt as he approached, its tail wobbling against the chill breeze. "Come, child," he coaxed, unwinding the rope. The lamb followed, bleating as it twisted the rope against Edwin's firm grip.

Whispering a prayer, he slipped the rope from the lamb's neck and, using his knee to brace the soft creature against the ground, tied the rope firmly around each pair of legs.

The lamb screamed, writhing against the sudden confinement. Edwin loathed this part. But it had to be done. For her, he would do anything.

Pulling the bullet from his pocket, he pushed it into place. The rifle's stock pressed firmly into his shoulder, and its cool wood grazed his face.

The lamb tilted its face up, toward him. Edwin acknowledged the open mouth and the wavering tongue, but he no longer heard the cries. He positioned the dark metal straight against the soft white fur and took one last look into a pair of wide, terrified eyes.

With a zing and a crack, it was done. The head slumped to the ground, the eyes open but unmoving. Edwin breathed, several long breaths.

He leaned the rifle against the outer wall and reached for his blade. Kneeling, he pressed and sawed into the thick, resistant neck until the blood seeped through. Dragging the small animal toward the hook, he hoped it wasn't too late. Edwin couldn't wait another week.

"She's here," he called to the night. "Please, hurry."

It would be a while yet. It always took a while; he didn't know why. But it did, and rather than sit and wait while the carcass bled, better to just keep prepping.

Returning inside, he rested the rifle behind the tool chest, away from view. Edwin rubbed a bar of lye against his hands and then into the grain of the table. It was a solid table at least—a gift from Ilana's father. They were from this place. Edwin wasn't. He used to work for Lord Strathcona himself, and they'd detoured through this small valley entirely by accident. Smitten by the lovely young woman with the wavy chestnut hair, he'd simply let the caravan leave without him, abandoning the riches of his former life for the soft words of a kind woman. If he'd known then . . . well, it didn't matter now.

He mustn't lose this chance. Back outside, he scanned the forest as the water pumped into the oversize bucket. Lugging it inside, he poured the cool water over the soapy table, the suds flowing to the ground, washing over the blood-stained floor. Hurrying, he cut off a measure of twine, grabbed a sturdy hook, and picked up his blade.

The twine was for tying off the ends he didn't care to contemplate. The hook was for the guts. In his father's old shop, they'd used the offal for sausage. Edwin couldn't see to do it. Instead, he left the plump, glossy innards out, for the forest to take. He slogged outside and squatted over the furry mass.

Edwin yanked, again and again with the hook, concern suffusing his expression as the twilight faded to darkness. Reaching for his saw, he noticed her. He exhaled.

The lamb was more beautiful now than in life. Her long legs gleamed in the darkness, her ears and snout alive and twitching. Her eyes flitted about the dark forest, oblivious to her own glistening remains strewn at Edwin's feet, illuminated by the moonlight. Edwin stretched an imploring hand toward her, then dropped it to his side; there was no apology he could offer.

There was only Rachel.

He glanced wistfully back at the carcass. He hadn't moved with enough haste, and she wasn't quite ready to tie up. Bleeding would have to wait. The meat might suffer, but he had ways around that. He placed the saw onto a mound of dirt.

"I'm ready," he said, his voice quavering.

The lamb took tentative steps forward, first walking, then leaping back and forth in little jolts. She darted into the trees.

Edwin shielded his face as they tromped through the thick undergrowth of the woods. Branches snapped against his hands, and cobwebs caught in his fingers. He wished they'd just take the path, but the little ones never did. When he finally emerged into the field, two large silhouettes loomed against the dark, cloudy sky.

The curling branches of the mayor's tree contrasted the sharp lines of the steeple to its side. The top limbs, where the bark had fallen, glowed almost white, even in the darkness. With a shudder, he forced his eyes from the harrowing tree. He broke into a run as shapes emerged around him. Lambs and calves danced in all directions, radiant and free, their bellowing and bleating combining in a chorus of harmony and life.

Where was she? She had to be here. She must be here.

Rachel.

She never saw him, the way the others did. It didn't matter. He absorbed her sweet expression, a tiny image of Ilana. Her hair swung to each side in two glowing braids. As she danced, her cotton dress swished underneath the apron, so lovingly embroidered. She twirled a nosegay of columbines—oh, he'd have to tell Ilana that—until, with a start, she raced toward him.

No, not toward him. He turned as the spring lamb rushed from behind him toward the little girl. She fell to her knees, letting the flowers scatter beneath the slender hooves. She nuzzled her tiny face into the creature's soft wool.

Edwin gazed, transfixed, as tears streamed down his ruddy cheeks.

Without warning, they disappeared. "No!" he shouted. "No!" Realization dawning, he dropped to the ground, watching in horror as the moon broke through the drifting clouds, streams of moonlight illuminating the tall, geometric, steeple.

He dug his thick fingers into the dirt, where the flowers had never really been. He choked back his tears. He'd seen her. It was enough.

Edwin, stood, wavering, to his feet. Best to be back. There was skinning to do, and he hadn't even bled the creature properly.

It was Sunday night, after all, and Mr. Harper would be by bright and early for his chops.

"I love you," Edwin whispered. "And I will never leave."

November Bridge

We'll keep with the sad and surreal for one more story before we switch back to some humor.

The brewery in my hometown has an annual writing contest (a really fun idea for its patrons!), and the Winter 2019 theme asked for stories inspired by a specific beer that they sell. Many of their beers have humorous names that evoke all kinds of big characters and adventure, but I immediately knew which beer I'd choose: The Milford Pub Ale.

I wrote about the literal location of their pub in Milford, an old, historical part of the village, and a place involved in several of the events of my life. And not just my life—this location was frequently referenced in the first book (of length, after *Rules are Rules* at age 7) I'd written at age 16, a history of Milford from the perspective of children: *Echoes of Laughter*. I have many memories, happy and bittersweet, at this location over the years. It is also a location of terrible events from my youth that don't feel right to spell out here, especially with my CPTSD. And thus I was drawn to write this piece, a composite of a great many things in a small space. Though it might not overtly read this way, to me it is magical realism. Truly, it is the most *Milford* piece I could have written. Even if it's a little heavy for the brewery contest. As it turned out.

The night of the awards was strange. Not only did it highlight how *much* I did not fit in, not anymore, not with the crowd (though the brewery and its staff are lovely), not with the other stories submitted (some were outright offensive), but I was told that someone who had lived there a while understood one of the references in the story, and explained it to the rest of the staff. It all felt surreal, though I enjoyed a really good beer and the company of my friends.

I did win an honorable mention.

Everyone my age from my hometown who has read this has burst into tears. So, for you, Milford '94.

Content note for sadness, and for anyone who knows the reference.

Inspired by Milford Pub Ale

SHE sat there, at the little park off of Main, as the sun set over the river. It was warm for early November, which wasn't warm at all, and with her ears covered and fingers buried in her pockets, she could stay here just a while longer to watch the last colors drain from the sky and the sparkles of night emerge. Her bottom felt cold against the bench, the modern sort with coated seats whose ridges felt bumpy even against her thick sweatpants.

A splash sounded against the water, rolling under the rounded bridge. Her grandfather used to tell stories of the old bridge, of jumping off into the summer water with howls of joy and the taunts of the other boys. It wasn't safe, of course. Just as she and her friends had walked along the worn tracks, keeping their ears peeled for the sound of a distant train. Her own grandchildren would never do these things; they were safe at home, inside before dark.

She'd always stayed out.

Turning in her seat, she shifted to watch the light stream from the park beyond, filtering over a lone, drooping willow. The park was different, too. Clean and joyful, you could see across now, to the games, and the trees, and almost to the rings beyond where families sat in the summer for concerts.

There was old sadness that way, hidden in the wet leaves. The sadness wasn't talked about, and maybe it shouldn't be, but people knew. She knew.

Her eyes wandered across the water, to the gold glow of the brewery up the hill. She was glad to see it; like a halo over a sacred place, it brought something back to a spot where people were meant to gather. Where they always had.

She watched the groups seated across the long patio, turning on heaters for extra warmth and raising their glasses in toast. Joy. Companionship. *Home.* For a moment, she considered walking up, aside the metal rail and through the quiet parking lot. Maybe someone would see her there. Know her. Remember who she'd been.

But, instead, she stayed in the park, and rose from the cold, hard table to sit in the chilly grass. Leaning back, she nestled her head back against the soft ground and watched as the sky turned to inky dark and the stars pricked through, twinkling in greeting. Finally closing her eyes, she listened to the ripples of the water and the laughter up the hill, absorbing each sound and wishing she could join them on the patio, just for a while.

You see, she wasn't really there.

Her Majesty, Dawn

The next three stories were submitted in 2018, for a spec-fic anthology of women in leadership roles going into battle. As I've *always* written about women leaders, and I had just taken a turn away from writing violence, I found myself pulling immediately to satire. I actually wrote three stories in a row, including the next two in this collection (and one I didn't submit or include here, though I also like it), in a satirical style. Finally, forcing myself to write something serious so I had a chance, I came up with the tale of a dragon, "Szlnaya", which completes this trio. I had a hard time deciding which to pick. This next story was my favorite. The following story was my editor, Camille's favorite, and the last one was favored by Chris. So I submitted all three, but as you can see, they all ended up here. I hope you enjoy my efforts.

And as it will be entirely obvious to those who know, these were clearly submitted to Mad Scientist Journal, because they require a 1st person narrative by a fictional author, along with the bio of that author. I prefer writing in 3rd person, but I did my best.

I bore a great responsibility that day, having been entrusted with the ominous and dreadful Sphere of Storms.

The Sphere held the power to destroy nations. To destroy the sky itself. Yet, I, a simple burrower, could not be tempted by its evil pulses and whispering thoughts, for storms destroy the burrows. And I like the burrows.

Thus, it was entrusted into my sturdy side pack for the trip through the Great Woods to seek passage and assistance from Her Majesty, the Queen of the Elves.

"Why must we find Her Majesty again?" I asked, not burdened by the weight of the powerful Sphere, yet missing my friends at the burrows.

The wizard, Fanathar, slammed his staff onto the path. "The object of which we must not speak is evil beyond measure. Only Her Majesty, Dawn of the Blessed Eternal Morning of the Ancient and Lost Forest Home, can grant us passage and favor to banish the Sphere in the grim lands beyond."

Beside him, Ilian, the lone elf amongst us, bowed his head in reverence.

"Now, small being," Fanathar declared, "speak not of this object again or I may be tempted to unleash its fury."

So, I wasn't exactly sure why he kept suggesting he might use the Sphere. This did give me incentive to keep the object zippered tight in my pack. I resolved not to bring it back up.

"I dread being in her presence," Pantos said. The human's broad hand clasped his sheathed sword.

Sometimes I cannot escape my own curiosity on comments that don't seem to make sense. Perhaps this is attributed to my innocence.

"Why's that?" I asked.

Pantos snorted. "Everyone says she's bossy."

"It's true," Ygran said, his gruff voice sounding from beside me, where his stature did not much exceed my own. "She speaks and expects everyone to drop whatever they are doing to address her commands."

I almost asked why that would be unexpected for the Queen of All Beings, but perhaps my innocence biased my thoughts.

Together, we plodded ahead.

Around us, the light faded as the trees of the forest grew

taller and wider, and the canopy above wove into patterns of a thick blanket, like the one in my burrow.

A chill set within my bones as I wondered how close we were to the elves' magical forest glen. Their sacred home.

I was pretty excited to see it.

Bump, a grass-planter back in my village, used to go on about the elf home, and Ilian, here, he flushed up at every mention of the place. I was thinking it had to be pretty neat.

Above, lightning cracked. Fanathar raised his staff in terror and Pantos swung his sword in a wild circle. Just in case, I ducked.

"Fanathar! It's a forest rain," I reassured him. "The, uh, terrible object is secure."

"Do not tempt me, small one," he whispered.

The rain lasted not much longer than nightfall, and the sun was rising once again when a large sparkling arch drew into view. Ilian closed his eyes, speaking in a strange language.

"I hope she's in a good mood," Ygran growled.

"Yeah, I don't know if that's relevant," I offered, but the others were fixated on the gates ahead.

As we walked through, a magic veil lifted and we were suddenly on a bridge made of pure glitter, leading to a tower laced with winding green and silver vines.

At this point, I was ready to meet the Queen.

Guards opened a tall set of doors, and together, we walked in. An elf sat at a desk, chewing on a pen.

"Are we expecting you?" he asked.

Fanathar stepped forward. "I am the wizard Fanathar. We bear an object of such dire consequence that I can only speak of it to Her Majesty, Dawn of the Blessed Eternal Morning of the Ancient and Lost Forest Home."

"Ok, so no appointment then," the elf sighed. "She's under an open-door policy, but I'm going to need to reshuffle you to the morn, when—" He paused, placing a hand over his pointed ear. "Ok, she says come in." The elf shrugged.

A second elf appeared in the far doorway and led us down a passageway trimmed with patterns of gold. Real gold, I'd bet.

"Weapons here," she said, pointing to a wide bench.

"Do as commanded," Fanathar said, as everyone but I, for I carry no weapons, laid their devices down on the bench.

Feeling nervous about the Sphere of Storms in my pack, I started to unclip the buckle.

"No!" Fanathar hissed. "Would you tempt me to unleash the Storm upon us here, ending all being and untying the threads of eternity?"

I kept the pack on.

He led us into a room where an elf stood at a tall desk, writing something with a glittery branch. She wore black pants and a green tunic. Gray, curly hair was pulled up in a bun, secured with a golden coil of wire.

"Please, come in. I've got a hard stop in about ten ticks. What can I do for you?"

"Er, yes," Fanathar said. "We're looking for Her Majesty, Dawn of the Et—"

"Yes, hi, I'm Dawn," the elf interrupted, extending her hand. Seeing Fanathar was too flustered to shake it, she dropped it back to her side.

"Her Majesty? Born of the line of Divine Royalty?" Fanathar sputtered.

"No," she said, setting a pair of reading glasses onto her desk. "Actually I started in engineering. Worked my way up the sacred tree for about ten thousand years and then took over when Moon Dust retired."

Ilian dropped to his knees, murmuring. She rested the branch next to her glasses and walked over. "No, please, get up. Forest Elf? I've got family in Ala'myr'na'dion if you're from that way. Beautiful country."

"My Lady," he stammered.

Dawn glanced at a glittering hourglass on her desk. "Questers, right? Are you looking for passage? We're not really ticketing right now with annuals due, so as long as you're not putting anyone in danger, I'd say just . . . go forth."

"I'm carrying the Sphere of Storms," I blurted.

Pantos roared, reaching for his sword, which thankfully was back in the hallway, causing him to instead perform a sort of air flourish. Fanathar stepped forward, his arms extended wide in front of Pantos.

"Forgive us, Lady Queen, for not speaking of this dire object. I have enlisted a creature of supreme innocence to bear its burden so I would not be tempted to unleash the Eternal Storm!" By this point, the wizard was shouting.

The door opened and the elf who had escorted us popped her face inside. "Ma'am, you have a call on the Basin of All Seas, if you'd like to take it?"

Dawn waved a hand. "I'm good, Stace." The door clicked shut behind her and the Queen turned to me with a small smile.

"They don't ask you to take the minutes, do they?"

I wasn't sure what that meant. The Queen turned back to Fanathar, her voice calm.

"A couple of things. First, let's get you on my calendar to discuss some alternative quest paths for your companion. I'd like to see some more varied skill-building, as innocence is considered outside of our professional evaluation boundaries.

"Next, you mentioned wanting to unleash the End Storm. That might give some the impression that you were considering ending life for eternity and that maybe it's best for you not to continue through the sacred forest. Let me ask you: What do *you* think?"

Fanathar looked abashed but Pantos shook his head. "The Sphere of Storms is an evil object, Your Majesty."

Something told me the Queen of Elves probably knew that, but she smiled politely.

"Yes, and I'd prefer not to risk sending you into the sacred woods, let alone the grim plains, with it. Here's what I'm—"

"We can't just do nothing!" Ygran shouted, with Ilian nodding in agreement.

"Right," Dawn continued, "so here's what I'm—"

"I'll lay down my life if it means—" Pantos raised his fist.

"*Team,*" Dawn interrupted, with a punctuating spark of green lightning that seemed to get the group's attention. "Here's what I'm thinking. Since you've done us the service of finding this long-lost dark orb, let's go ahead and destroy it now, and then you can all go back to your homes." She looked at me. "Wouldn't you agree?"

My smile told her that I definitely did.

"Destroy it?" Ilian stood taller. "Team, if we could destroy the Sphere, our quest would be completed—we could return to our homes!"

I was pretty sure Dawn had just said that, but the others whooped and cheered.

Fanathar gazed at my pack as though channeling see-through vision. I hoped he did not have see-through vision. "If only we knew how to destroy this foul artifact," he mused.

"Yes, so, fortunately I am Queen of the Elves," Dawn said, grabbing the long, banded twig from her desk. "Stace," she called.

The assistant popped back into the room. "Could you get one of the snack bags, please?"

A moment later, the elf returned with a large cloth bag. Dawn reached her hand toward me, and I trusted her.

If she was Queen of the Elves, it was for a good reason. With a zip of my little pack, I handed her the Sphere. Within it, sparks crackled and jumped.

As Fanathar's eyes began to widen, Dawn slipped the Sphere into the bag, rolled the top closed, placed it onto the ground, and then stomped on it. Glass shattered into shards inside, and I thought I heard a muted scream. A dark mist emerged into the room, and singing a low series of incantations, Dawn waved the wooden twig in a curved pattern, clearing the air.

"Well, that should do it. *Ugh*," she said, glancing at the hourglass. "I've kept the Dwarf Queen waiting. I need to run. Really nice to meet you. Stace will get you a port back. Best wishes, and don't hesitate to reach out if I can help."

With a grin in my direction, Her Majesty, Dawn of the Blessed Eternal Morning of the Ancient and Lost Forest Home was gone in a flash of light.

Moments later, I was glad to return to my burrow, where my friends rushed to greet me, happy that I was safe.

Tuft of West Canton lives in a burrow on the east side of the peaceful Frog Lake. They enjoy a life of sunshine and befriending the birds of their breezy orchards, except such times when they are called upon for epic greatness. They have established a lasting friendship with Her Majesty, Dawn, who sometimes invites Tuft for game night at the enchanted forest.

ladies' Night at Fozwock's

After satire, I tried humor. So here's my battle story of mild ribaldry. Enjoy.

Content note for alcohol.

J spent a month conjuring the fake ID that would get me into Fozwock's.

There is no better place in the thirteen kingdoms to catch a connection to the fast track than this little hole in the wall behind the Tower of the High Council. If you don't know that, you're not paying attention.

Only issue is I'm seventeen. And you gotta be *twenty* to get in.

Now, I don't know what wand pusher came up with the idea that I can't sit down for a vial of good potion, but my cousin Prithley, who still asks his dates to ride a *broomstick* around town with him, is all set. I'm not discounting age as a factor, but then they shouldn't discount *me*.

I think I got this, though.

With no more time to spare, I slipped the little card into my embroidered wallet and took a good look at myself in the mirror. *Witch's cap, dark makeup, sheer blouse.*

Wait.

No one looks this good after work.

Muttering, I tossed off the cap, did a half-wand job of wiping off all my makeup, and threw on a WitchCon hoodie over my robe.

Yes, now I looked like an intern. A *twenty-year-old intern.* Maybe even twenty-one.

A quick port later, I was cruising the alley between the tall curvy stone walls, casually wandering past Fozwock's and trying to walk like it wasn't my first stop of the night. Seeing the guards, I turned as if I'd heard someone calling me from inside. With a shrug, like I didn't really want to go in, I ambled toward the door. A neon sign blinked: *Ladies' Night.*

Oh, great. I timed tonight for the peak of the High Council session, but I didn't know they had *ladies' night* here. Well, it's Wednesday. So not all the leaders are here, then? I thought about turning around. Tomorrow might be—

"ID, Lady," the guard grunted, wearing a rhinestone collar and glowing UV lip gloss. *Ok. Maybe I'm out of my league.*

No, all in now. I'm not getting interrogated by jail demons over this, and no one is telling my moms. They have enough going on.

I flipped the card out, flicking it between my fingers. The guard raised a wand and ran it over the ID. Grunting, she tapped it and turned it over again.

I worked a month on this; it better not crap out now.

"She's with me," a deep voice said behind me, grabbing the card from the guard's hand and yanking me in by my sleeve.

And this was the moment I found myself face-to-face with Ezbelle, Forest High Witch.

At least that's what her badge said. Seeing my eyes on it, she flipped off the lanyard and dropped it into her coat.

"You missed spectral," she said. "New spectral 'chant on IDs gives them a classified prism effect under club lights. They were almost on to you."

"Um, thanks," I said, feeling embarrassed. "Why'd you let me in?"

"It was a good attempt. I respect that. I can use more smart kids in Forest Ops. Now, don't network me yet; I need a cold drink and a hot witch. Then we'll talk."

What?

Within about ten minutes, Ezbelle was making out with a lanky witch, and I decided to go order a drink. Luckily, since I was already let in, they didn't ask for ID.

"Don't take it personal," the bartender said.

"Huh?"

"Forest witch; you're not her type. Too clean."

"Oh, ok. Well, could I get a small cauldron, then? Whatever's, uh, on the house." I thought that was how you said it; I couldn't afford something pricey.

The bartender cut me a glare, so I pulled all my coins from my purse. Relaxing, she said, "Yeah, one house cauldron, coming up. Call it that next time."

Cauldron in hand and purse empty, I wandered back toward the tables. A dwarf was leaned back against a thick wood table, her arms stretched wide, revealing a golden bodice. A shield rested against the pillar behind her, with a thick canvas jacket draped over it.

"Have a seat," she said with a nod, pointing at the bench next to her.

"Clan Leader—" I began.

"Please. Tina," she corrected. "Long day, huh? Where were *you* stuck?"

"Me, oh, I was running around. And, uh, you?"

"Nothing big. Just had to negotiate a mining bill between

three bleeping* dwarf kings while trying not to let on that my secretary *quit* yesterday because some provincial firm gave her an inflated raise that they'll drop in a year once they've worked her for everything she knows about my five-year strategic plan, which she helped *proofread* as if that means she's going to understand its ins and outs."

(*So, Tina used words I just cannot repeat. Like, a lot of them. But you get the idea.)

"Oh, wow, well, sounds like you did a great job," I said, trying not to cough on a wave of green haze that floated up from my cauldron.

Then I saw her.

I mean, it had to be her. Bleeping* Sorceress Janai, head of all witchcraft for the entire seven kingdoms. (*Sorry, Tina sorta rubbed off on me.)

That's when I noticed Ezbelle was nowhere to be seen, and the guard from the door was over talking to the bartender. And they were both looking my way. *Uh oh.*

No, I got this.

Maybe if I hadn't been afraid of getting thrown out into the alley, I would have just stared and stammered at Janai until she ported back home. But I knew I might not get this chance again. And I was not letting that float away.

Sidling up to the long table where Janai had tossed aside her amazing black hat, I downed what was left of my cauldron. In fact, I don't know what a house cauldron is supposed to be made of, but I *may* have left too big of a tip. I was feeling bold. Like, real bold.

"Um, hi," I said. "I'd buy you a cauldron, but then you'd think I was trying to win your favor through unscrupulous means."

Janai smirked. "Are you?"

"High Sorceress, I am trying to win your favor through overt and unabashed means." I hiccupped.

"How'd you get in?" she asked. Or, really, commanded. It wasn't so much of a question.

"Enchanted an ID. Missed the new spectrum chant, but Ezbelle snuck me in."

"Good Wizards," Janai muttered. "Are you ok?"

"What? Oh, her. No, it's ok."

Janai looked relieved.

"Can I see it?"

See it? Right. I handed her the ID. She didn't even wave a wand or anything. Just peered at it and passed it back.

"Not bad. What did you say your name was?"

"Kazel."

A siren had taken up on the small, smoky stage, and Janai looked like she was gathering her things to leave.

"I'm studying enchantment." I hurried to get the words out. "I'd like to learn from you directly." Thinking that was too much, I added, "It's my passion." I flashed what I hoped to be an endearing smile.

Janai's hand stopped rummaging through her bag, and she looked at me with sort of sad eyes. "It's not what you kids think," she said. "It's long days. It's hearing lies yet knowing that arguing against them just gives them wind. It's carrying everyone's secrets, pain, and sorrow. It's giving bad news to people you've grown to love and having them resent you for it.

"Spells? Only occasionally and only when someone remembers how goddess-blessed *good* you are at it." She pushed aside an empty vial. "Now, all that. You wouldn't want that, would you?"

Her words were spinning in my mind, and maybe now that cauldron was too. "I can do it," was all I said.

Janai's smile was warm but her eyes were still distant. "Hey. I'll walk you out. Get home. Avoid the demons. And get back to school. Work your pointy little cap off and apply for enchantment during trials. You make it in, and . . . I'll remember you. Ok?"

I didn't know what to say, especially under the guards' knowing glare as Janai walked me back out into the street and whipped a quick portal between us. With a wink, she was gone.

I guess I wasted my night after all.

Kazel Meadowwalker is a serious witch, originally from Outwood Glen East. She is finishing her degree in enchantment from University of the Second Kingdom, after which she hopes to take over the world. She enjoys embroidery and rainstorms.

Szlnaya

Again, I knew I needed to give them something serious to consider. And I know this one was considered. But it's all good, because you can now enjoy my battling dragon story here.

Content note for fire and off-page death.

I heard his cries from within a dream.

Stretching my wings from the safety of my wide pine grove, I opened my eyes, trying to decide if the cries had been real.

They felt real. "Tyk," I whispered. He did not answer.

I rose onto my hind legs. Unless the voice was a memory, then it came from somewhere. Yes, a pull. Toward the east, toward the lands where they lived.

Cool water pooled in a rock by the stream, and I lapped a long drink, trying to clear my mind. The echo was still there. I could no longer hear his cries, but the sensation drew me toward him.

I must help him.

I knew that if his danger were great enough to reach me here, I could not go alone. I was valuable to the other small ones. My black, scaled hide was worth many of their villages—to many, worth those villagers' lives.

Who would travel with me to such darkness?

I was about to find out.

I stopped, remembering my egg, nestled in its bed of mud and soft needles. I had lived so many years on my own or with partners of passing interest that I sometimes forgot the egg resting beside me. Soft and vulnerable, I couldn't leave it alone.

Tyk's cries rang in my mind. They were real; I was certain.

A deep growl of resignation bubbling through my throat, I lifted the egg and cradled it in my arms. "You're coming with me."

I flew over my own valley, pangs pulsing in my heart as I left its tall trees, tiny creatures, and clustered flowers.

Humming to my egg, as I had taken to doing, I flew range after range until I reached the sacred place of gathering: Kzaan's Ledge.

Swooping down toward its vast plateau of parched rock, I pulled back my neck, and with all the force I knew how to muster, I let loose a distress scream fit for the dracas of lore.

Upon landing, I switched the egg to my other arm, for I was not used to carrying it.

The wind grew and swirled as they joined me, one by one, every dragon of ability within range, as the old ways dictated.

They would not be happy when they heard my plea. I resolved to bear the consequence.

Tyk was my friend. And I would not leave him to die.

Waves of sand pelted my scales as the scores of dragons landed around me, their thick wings pounding the air with concussive beats that rang in my ears like a welcome rain. I drew my wing in around the egg, just in case.

The ground rumbled underneath me as the others waited for my plea. My decision made, I raised my head.

"I am Szlnaya. My friend is in distress and I am called by the ancient magic to save him. He rests in a place I dare not go alone. The land of . . . Humanity."

I gripped the stones to brace against the stomps of claws and wished I could block my ears from the deafening roars of their fury.

"What dragon has ventured beyond our lands?" one called, fire welling from his teeth.

"He is not a dragon. He is . . . human."

This brought a moment of pure silence, broken by an outburst of jeers. "Which ancient magic connects you to humans?" They laughed.

I was not ashamed of my answer. "The magic of Heart," I said, baring my teeth. "He is my friend."

They stomped and laughed around me, and the air filled with their smoke. I breathed in deep.

"As I said, he is my friend. I call him Tyk."

"It has no *name*," another mocked. "This is just a name you have given it."

This was true. But I could not just call him *man*.

"He is in danger," I repeated, standing taller. "I call for assistance."

"We will save no *human*," they screeched, almost in chorus.

I waited until the clamor subsided, waited until they would hear what I had to say. "Then I will go alone. I will go alone, knowing that my kind no longer respond to calls of distress. That the ancient magic of Heart is not just dead among Humanity, but among Dragonkind as well."

Uneasy, I considered whether it was true. That I would go alone. I looked at the egg in my arms.

"I will join you," a voice called, as a small maroon drake pushed through the crowd. Another followed him, almost as young. I wondered at my wisdom. Would I lead a band of youth into peril?

"And I," another called, this one older.

The cries deafened in my ears as not a mere few, but a sizable band of dragons took their places on the ledge, ready to push off into flight.

Pushing to their front, I gripped my egg securely, and howled my best call of action, ignoring the scores who lingered behind. I launched into the sky, my wings strong and wide.

Behind me, a wedge of dragons grew, like a flower unfurling across the gray clouds, with petals of bright color.

And hope.

I led them forward, the cries growing stronger in my mind. *Tyk*, I called. *We are coming.*

There was no doubt where our quest led. A pillar of thick, black smoke rose from the forest outside of a large, walled city. The humans gathered outside their own walls, watching the blaze of burning timbers yet keeping a distance from it.

I could not blame them for not saving my Tyk. Their tiny bodies wrapped with thin membranes would not survive even moments within the billowing blaze.

Tyk. I no longer felt his cries. Yet I would not leave. Not until I knew.

As we approached, panic erupted, and I lost my sympathy for the little animals. During the span of our descent, they ran for their instruments of attack—tying the ropes of large, wheeled shooters to frightened horses who dragged them our way.

I could not let my kin land here. The humans' beads of

metal would break bones or damage an eye. Even their little blades could pierce our thick skin if stabbed or thrown with skill. I could not have landed, were I alone.

Turning in flight, I held the egg close.

"Hold an arc here," I commanded. "Each of you, two tails apart. Create a wall of flame, five tails from the forest line. Do not move toward the humans, just hold them from me. I will be fast," I added, knowing how tiring it was to hold position mid-air, as well as to maintain a stream of fire.

Without question, they blasted their flames, almost blowing me backward from the sheer force. By instinct, I roared as loud as I was able, up into the sky. If Tyk still lived, I hoped he would hear me and know I was close.

I could not fly through the pillar of black smoke above the forest. Preparing to run through the burning trees, I started to lower myself into the space between the walls of dragon flame and forest fire. I froze, hovering in place. *The egg.* It enjoyed a nice flame bath, but I had not had an egg before. Could it withstand a sustained inferno such as the one before me?

There was no time left to deliberate, so I closed my eyes and let the choices flash in my mind. The egg was small. Innocent.

Struck by a connection, I swooped toward the maroon drake, the first who had stepped forward. I motioned for him to follow. We landed together, and I reached forward with the egg. "Would you protect this? For me?"

"Perhaps we will be friends," he said, reaching to cradle the egg in two lanky arms. I did not know whether he meant me, or the hatchling who may later emerge, but I bowed in gratitude before turning on my claws to face the forest beyond.

Darting forward and squinting through my almost-closed

eyes, I focused only on two things: First, keeping as far as I could from the whitest fire, and second, focusing with all my energy on the magic of Heart, the magic that had allowed Tyk to call me here.

Through dancing orange flames and pillars of char, I felt him ahead. Or, not him, but a place I should be.

Kicking down the faltering walls of a wooden dwelling, I stomped through, the heat beginning to sear at my scales and burn in my ears. Sparks sputtering from my mouth, I saw Tyk, alone in a room, his body curled in a rounded shape behind layers of human accessories which he had knocked onto themselves to form little barriers from the fire. I pushed them away.

Tyk was dead, and not newly.

Then, had I wasted my call of distress? Would the egg and I return to Black Crest alone, scorned for our—

His shape reminded me of an egg. Like my egg. I peeled him away, taking one last look at his unseeing eyes, and a ball emerged below him, a brown-skinned child in a thin white cloth, like a little flower that had bloomed under a rock.

Her face streaked with mud and tears and her hair full of ash, she did not cry but stared up at me with eyes wide with terror. Her skin bore scratches and burns; she started to cough from the smoke, now that I had uncovered her.

Like the egg, I could not carry her through this fire.

Whisking her into my arms, I crouched as low as I could, wrapping my arms around the little bundle. With a howl so bellowing that I hoped Tyk could hear it from his past, I shot upward, through the missing roof and past the burning trees and catapulted into the cloud above.

Still unwilling to expose the child to the searing smoke, I

wrapped my wings around her and turned my body in a spiral, pushing as far away as I could. As I plummeted back toward the burning treetops, only then did I take the risk that I must, opening both wings and flying, with all speed that I could gather, back toward the wall of dragon flame.

With a bump, I landed, fretting at the child's cuts. If I could leave her close to other humans, they would know how to care for her.

"Thank you," I called to the maroon drake, who reached out with my egg. Taking the egg and the child together in my arms, I called to the others. Their flame barrier was faltering, and I could see that their wings wavered, tired, in the smoky air.

"Cease fire. Withdraw upward," I ordered.

I was glad to see that the child covered her ears. I wondered if I was loud to my egg.

As we flew closer, I saw the gathering of humans in detail. Their rocks launched at us from tree-hewn devices, and the horses screamed in fear and pulled at the ropes around their necks.

I held the child close, sensing her terror.

Was it for me? Or for them?

Unsure, I called one last time to the others. "Return in safety to your homes. My call is answered. Gratitude is mine. Honor is yours."

The pledge resolved, there was no need to remain. Line after line of dragons peeled away to their homes and soon I was alone again, flying westward with aching limbs.

Landing within my pine grove, I set the egg back into its bed of mud and soft needles. I placed my claw on its soft surface and laid an ear on its side, seeking a sign it hadn't taken harm from the journey. Breathing in relief, I felt it moving from within as it seemed to snuggle back into position. I lifted away.

The child made little whimpering noises within my grasp, like a birdsong. I set her down next to the creek, pulling cool water into my mouth and letting it run down over her dusty hair and arms.

I rested a claw, as lightly as I could, on her back, and held it there as her shaking subsided. Not knowing what she would eat, I flew to find some fruit and placed it at her feet. She pulled one within her little round mouth, and with bones that could barely be called teeth, she began to chew at the soft pulp.

In her eyes, something familiar touched me.

Perhaps, Tyk was not dead after all.

Szlnaya of Black Crest was born during the Age of Fire. She spent much of her youth exploring all the Lands of One, but more recently she has found her calling nurturing the smaller creatures of her home valley. She has recently taken in an egg and a human child and is unsure how much change this will bring.

Jhe Museum of Gultural Gomfort

Ok, this is an odd one (I know, they are mostly odd) because it was written in early April 2020, in the early peak of the pandemic and during relative lockdown. My friend and I had been joking about quite offensive items showing up on Facebook Marketplace *(that cookie jar!)*, and people perhaps wondering why they had no offers. We joked about a fake museum where you could take these awful things, and get them out of circulation by soothing people of privilege who felt bad throwing them out. But right after, I had a severe mental health collapse, and for a time I was focused on recovering. By the time I got back to this story in early summer, after the murder of George Floyd and resultant swells to movements, some of this was sort of *happening*, at least at the corporate and government level, toppling bullshit statues and with racist logos being finally chucked away. Despite being urged to submit this, in that climate, I simply couldn't. It could be read as a statement on those events. Things were too important and there were too many layers and I didn't want anyone getting the wrong message regarding my intent—it was important to view the appeasement as satire, and I just didn't think I was someone who could be saying anything with humor in that environment. (If you are reading this someday in the future and don't remember, it might be hard to convey how tense and layered 2020 really was.) But here, in the understanding of this collection and with context, I hope you enjoy our museum. Don't worry, we'll take great care of your items.

GAM settled into the plastic mesh chair, inspecting the old-fashioned book. Sometimes she grabbed one for a while before disposition; it passed the time in between visitors nicely. Nothing from the 21st century though—anything that made its way into the global information era should have known better. She recognized the flawed logic, but here was the certified place for it. Fact was, some of this 20th century stuff was really great, beyond the obvious issues.

It took a lot to shock her, honestly. Fifteen years at the Museum would steel the finest silk. Category 5.3, she droned to herself. *Animal products; non- skin/bone.* There was no point considering anymore whether she would have stayed remotely acceptable had she not clicked on that ad. Life ran and people followed.

She flipped to the back cover, a nice solid hardcover. She knocked against it for good measure. Oh, this did look great. Adventure, conflict, drama. Good quotes that didn't sound too forced. Let's see, probably glorifies war, women all fawning over the male MC, everyone is allocishetero and touching each other all the time without consent. Didn't look like a bloodline story, but you were never safe from a plot twist there. Bioessentialism bombs, she called them.

She turned to inspect the illustration on the front. Hopefully this was more one of those everyone-is-whitish deals as opposed to mistreated BIPOC. Then, she'd likely bail. "Ladies and Gentlemen," the author's preface began.

Chuckling, she turned the page. Oh, she loved the feel of a natural page.

Ring! The little desk chime sounded as the doors zipped open, and one of the usuals shuffled in, xyr steps echoing in the empty lobby. Not someone she recognized, to be clear, but the sort she was used to seeing. No intrigue today; maybe jewelry? Big sunglasses, thick coat—

Oh, I hope not. She peered at the coat, relieved to see it was just one of those poofy coats, cut for shape rather than wear. Of all the things Cam disliked carting back, it was big old fur coats. "Grandma treasured it so," they'd often implore. Well, then, Grandma could touch the thing.

Cam set down the book, scooting it out of sight under the ledge of the reception desk. She donned her smile.

"Welcome to the Museum of Cultural Comfort, Drop-Off Station 83. I'm Cam, she."

The client clutched at the coat, squeezing whatever it concealed like it might escape. "Jill, she," she managed to mutter out, while raising the sunglasses over her smooth hair. "Is this—"

"Yes, this is the drop-off for the Museum. Please don't be nervous; unless there's a timeframe issue, we're not looking for trouble."

The woman relaxed. A little.

That was the thing. Anyone did this job long enough, the idea of comforting people over knick-knacks that it was totally confusing why they still had really wore thin. But things went faster if the clients were at ease, so Cam smiled reassuringly.

Jill was still wired like taxidermy.

Cam leaned over the desk. "Is it Nazi?" Might as well be out with it if that's what they were dealing with. Every time she hoped she'd seen the last one, there was always someone else with a creepy story and a string of timeline absolutions.

"What!" Jill recoiled, clutching the coat.

Cam sighed. "Object brought back from 'the war'?" She braced for some story about how a trinket had been owned by the Emperor Himself, or Napoleon, or who cared, so they'd held onto it for the sake of history. Times were different back then. Cam didn't even argue with them anymore.

"No!"

Reaching down, Cam peeled off a sheet of paper and slid it out over the counter. Sometimes it was easier this way. "Main categories here on the left." She trailed her finger down the list, reading off a few. "Class Sports, Animal Products, Indigenous, Settler Indians, Antebellum Chic . . ." She wiggled the paper a little further out, coaxing the woman closer. Her finger stopped over Pandemic Folkware. Didn't need to invite that blech.

Jill's face scrunched. This time, Cam just waited.

"Sorry, but can I ask, but if you have Indigenous, what's a . . . *Settler Indian.*"

One thing Cam did not get into with clients was disposition, but she could certainly answer the question. "Indigenous covers artifacts belonging to indigenous people and nations. 'Settler Indian' is like, you know, grandma's ethereal 'brave' painting, cigar statues, pre-rise thanksgiving wares, twenty-c kids' toys, that sort of thing."

"Oh." Jill's hand twitched. "No, it's nothing like that." She paused. "Paper," she murmured.

"Right, off grid." Come on, everyone knew what paper was for. Cam glanced longingly at her novel as Jill stared off at the wall behind the desk.

"My grandpa treasured this."

"Mmm," Cam replied. "He passed on?"

Jill nodded.

"I'm sorry for your loss."

"Thanks."

Cam waited.

With a swoop of Jill's gloved hand, a tiny Carrie Fisher flew toward Cam, landing with Wonder Woman grace onto the metal counter. Slowly, Jill's hand released. Trembled. Drew back toward her body where it found her other hand in solidarity.

kaboom

"There, there," Cam said. "You're alright now."

"He said it was a collectible. There's a number." She pointed.

"It is. Yes, in very good shape too."

Cam forced herself to meet eyes with the Museum's newest guest. Defiantly, the tiny woman stared lustily upward—lips brushed with rose gold, body swirled in copper painted sculpture. *Chains.*

"It will be part of the collection? For history? But not with my name?"

"We'll take care of it. No name. You can rest assured that you did the right thing." She checked box 11.8 with a casual swipe, then tapped the bottom line.

"Oh, thank you." Grasping the pen, Jill initialed under Cam's finger, letting out a huge exhale then turning quickly to the side as Cam pushed her chair away. The pen clattered down, rolling to a stop against the figure's numbered base.

"Thank you," Jill repeated, stumbling backward through the empty lobby then turning as the door opened. With a familiar buzz, it closed again behind her. Reaching for the paper, Cam slid it into the slot for stats. Done and gone. Like so much should be. Except . . .

Cam tapped her book. The repatriation and research bins weren't due today, but trash always came at two. Humming her famous theme with deep melancholy because who could resist, Cam pinched up the tiny princess and carried her out into the large, empty warehouse.

WAVESCANNER

The next two stories are my earliest works in this collection. They are longer pieces, when not only was I just learning to write, but while I was in the midst of a great deal of life trauma and mental illness. I almost didn't include them because of both their weaknesses and also problematic elements, but I think they may be of interest to some of you, especially those who understand my origins and growth and appreciate my early writing for a variety of reasons. You may also note several uses of language I now champion against. I simply can't edit these at this point, because I just wouldn't write them now. So shooshing them over a bit would not accomplish anything meaningful. So, if you choose to skip these stories, you can flip past the next two, with my blessing. Otherwise, I invite you to stay along for the ride.

This first of the two, from June 2014, was my first anthology submission. It was for a collection by women authors, about women characters. I had this idea of unconventional superheroes. They were called the *Five Circles*, and first they'd each have a short story, then I'd write a novel about them all coming together to, I presume, save the world. I wrote this one first for the anthology, and it was not selected. Later, in September, when *The Banished Craft* was out for edits, I wrote the other four. Feedback I received from the inner circle was not positive, so I shelved the whole bunch. Which is good—the concept ties so closely to disability tropes and other problems; even with a full rewrite and revised concept it would be very complicated to do right. Even if I wanted to and decided I was the right person to try it, I no longer see myself writing superhero novels. Not when I can play to my strengths in quiet fantasy, with quiet heroes. Anyway, I've hesitantly included one of them here, because it was my first anthology submission and as we'll get to in a moment, it does speak to my state at the time.

I initially meant to include a second one, "Echofinder", because it was so absolutely strange and I was trying to be open and edgy, in defiance of my anxiety. But then when I re-read it, it had some pretty awesome concepts and flow, but it was *so offensive*, I couldn't even read it, let alone consider it. I couldn't even salvage an excerpt. Those of you who know me for my sensitivity reading would be shocked: I brushed over issues of drug use, abuse, gun violence, prison, race, and then I realized that the main character was Indigenous, and I gasped. I mean, it wasn't intentionally disparaging, it was just so . . . white. I guess the good piece of it is that if I have come *that far* in only six years, there is hope for our society yet.

And the rest of the *Five Circles* can stay unread, *Holy Prince*.

As for "Wavescanner", now that I understand my own mental disabilities better and the effort it was taking me at that time to hide them in a work environment where any mental health treatment was required to be reported and career-threatening, I at least can say this was written with a heavy measure of ownvoices, heartfelt intent, and personal *feeling*. And there's a cute romance. I hope its inclusion is worthwhile to you.

Content note for problematic treatment of disability with ableist language, and in relation to magic abilities.

cAT 11:18 this morning I realized that I might have to leave the apartment. I tapped the battered surface of my small kitchen table, and closed my eyes tightly, before opening them again. You see, I hate going out, nearly more than anything. Just thinking of being around people—wading through a sea of their thoughts—is unbearable.

But I had forgotten that, today at 1:00, Ms. Dovzhenko-Petit was scheduled to visit. She is an irritating woman, and yet she is the only person I am not allowed to ignore. As my social worker, she is required to check on me periodically to make sure that I am still meeting the right balance of well and not well. She sits in my kitchen and asks me pointed questions until she decides she can sign her papers, allowing her to leave me alone until the next visit.

And so, hesitantly I set the book I was reading down onto the table. A woman wielding a huge gleaming lance stared up at me, her hair windswept in a way that seemed entirely impractical. Nobody would fight with hair in their eyes, whipping around them. Not to mention leaving her chest exposed to attack the way that it was, putting it politely. But it was a good book so far, and I didn't want to leave it unfinished. But there was no way around it: I had to step out.

The toilet had broken a week or so ago. It is an old toilet, and barely worked, even as it was. I tried to reconnect the chain, which had slipped off, but I accidentally broke the plastic rod, that was apparently made out of some ancient plastic just waiting to die. Just my luck.

I meant to order a new part, but having been engrossed in a delightfully long story about an order of magic knights emerging from obscurity, the toilet repair had slipped my mind. I could flush it just fine by reaching back into the tank, but as Ms. Dovzhenko-Petit always took care to inspect the bathroom as the most likely place to observe improprieties, I couldn't risk it drawing her attention.

It was a simple repair, but as she would be here shortly, it was too late to have the rod shipped, even overnight. There was no way around it; I would need to run out and pick up the part myself.

Ms. Dovzhenko-Petit is the only person who could change my life. It is her job to certify that I am disabled enough to qualify for the housing benefit, but yet determine that I am capable enough to live on my own. Appearing disabled is no chore; Ms. Dovzhenko-Petit thinks I am nuttier than a macaroon every time I open my mouth. But convincing her I am fine to live alone takes a bit of attention.

An image formed in my mind of her tapping on the disconnected toilet handle with one hand—*click, click*—before returning to the kitchen to write in her oversized notepad. I could see the words scratched onto the paper: *Bathroom is non-functional. Recommend further review. Possible relocation.* I resigned myself and started to tie on my walking shoes.

Despite being, in some sense, my only real-life friend, Ms. Dovzhenko-Petit has never told me her first name. I suspect she believes that people like me are not on the same level as the public servants who monitor them. This is nonsense. I deserve respect for having to endure her evaluations at least as much as she does for conducting them.

Her last visit had not gone well. "Don't worry, I'm still disabled," I had offered, smiling, as she walked through the door. She scowled, but did not respond. This was fine; I was trying not to listen anyway. I held my dining chair out for her to sit in as she glanced around distastefully. Her eyes rested a long moment on the stacks of books in my bedroom.

"Those books, Nadine, they will gather dust. You need fresh air to breathe properly. If you'd like to donate them, I can arrange a pickup." I followed her gaze into the bedroom, where

I could see my books lining the walls like a sideways library without shelves.

"I keep them dusted." My eyes narrowed. I didn't want her touching my books. I love to read, mostly fantasy. When I'm reading, there is no buzzing in my mind. The characters tell me only the thoughts I should know, and otherwise leave me out of it.

Each evening, I walk around the room picking my books up and setting them down. I look at the covers, and I remember the way the characters made me feel. Sometimes I dream about joining them. Carrying a sword made of crystal, I would travel to the ends of the Earth and confront evil itself. "Thank you, Nadine," the High Wizard would say, with a low bow. "You have saved us all."

I was still holding the chair as Ms. Dovzhenko-Petit paused, and I heard her thinking that she ought to go check whether the books had reached a point of being considered unsanitary, but she didn't want to get dust on her new sweater. Which was ridiculous; she hadn't even taken her coat off.

She lowered herself into the chair, being careful not to lean against the back. She wrinkled her nose at the colorful unicorn illustration I had taped to my fridge. I tried not to smile.

"Yes, well, make sure the apartment stays tidy," she lectured. "As we've discussed, that's one reason that you could be relocated." *Relocated.* Her favorite word. Locked up. Committed. Whatever they call it now. Either way, I wasn't going.

"Nadine, please, have a seat," she had said in her business voice, holding her huge notepad in one hand while gesturing politely with the other toward the small kitchen table.

"Oh, I'm fine. Besides, I only have the one chair."

She cringed, and immediately her thoughts jumped to the list of reasons I was unstable. She began to recite them internally, as if practicing for the hearing. I tried not to react.

She finally left that day, after notifying me of the date that she would return. Which, as I noted, is today.

It is a delicate game we play. She thinks it is unsuitable for me to be living alone, and wants me "relocated" for my own good. Unfortunately for her, I've read the code governing disability situations—these things are all online, you see—and know the guidelines better than she does. There isn't a thing she can do to me. Except maybe if I have a broken toilet; that might be enough. I pulled on my favorite hoodie, as a tight feeling started to form in my gut.

I actually like living here. The day I moved in I started a new life, one where I could be alone, and didn't need to worry what other people would think of me. I remember the day my mother helped me move in. She had cried the whole time.

When she left, she gave me a quick, but powerful, hug. "I love you," she said. *I'm so sorry*, she thought, almost as if I were intended to hear that as well. She looked so scared. I wanted to try and ask her again what all of this meant, but I was scared too. Then her thoughts became jumbled. She was frightened of me, I guess. It was hard to say.

"I won't be able to visit much, Nadi. It is complicated." She stumbled over her words, as if they would no longer form.

In her thoughts, I caught something about protecting me, about not letting them find me. I knew my mother had secrets. After all these years together, I still didn't understand her constant fear, her evenings away from home, and her endless tears. But I could not ask her more. After all, I had promised.

I stared at her a moment, my heart cracking within my chest as I watched the tears gathering in her red eyes. She was beautiful, and warm, and soft, and I loved her with all of my being. But before I could hear more of her thoughts, or bring myself to ask another question, she squeezed my hand, and rushed away. I knew, within my core, she would not be visiting.

"Goodbye. I love you," I whispered. "Whatever it is, I am sorry too."

I was now alone, standing next to an old sign. It said, "West Side Apartments" next to a terrible etching of a palm tree. It was a dumb name, deserving of that ugly palm tree. But it is a nice enough apartment, especially once I understood that here, I could finally be alone.

I don't answer the phone on the rare occasion that it rings. I don't check the messages, and I've covered the little blinking light with a piece of electrical tape. I have an online book club subscription—it even gives you a discount. I found a grocery service online that would deliver food once a week, and I've checked the box on the form that says to leave it at the door if nobody answers.

It's a good life.

I put on my sunglasses and tried to shake out the knots in my stomach. It is a twenty-minute walk. If I was efficient I could get out of the store and back home with just enough time to install the rod into the toilet tank before Ms. Dovzhenko-Petit arrived. *You can do this*, I encouraged myself. I slung my backpack on and made my way down the steps to the courtyard below.

It felt sort of nice to be outside, really. Despite the bright sun, there was a slight chill to the air. But it was a nice chill. A plump red cardinal stared at me from a nearby tree. I wondered if I could hear what birds thought if I really tried. It was an interesting idea.

I took the back path to the shopping center. The street wound back and forth, around the small, understated houses. I passed a young woman, out pushing her baby in a carriage. She stayed on the other side of the street, and we passed without comment.

It has been like this nearly as long as I can remember. It had started when I first went to daycare. My mind would buzz and hum in interesting ways. I didn't realize what was happening until one day, my thoughts were interrupted by an overwhelming awareness of nausea. I didn't feel ill, yet I thought for certain that I was.

Confused, I looked around in time to see my friend CeCe become sick. I stepped back, afraid, wondering if I had caused it. But the teachers ignored me. They brushed past me as they rushed to assist with the little sick girl in front of me. One of them even stepped on my toe and didn't even think about it afterward. I moved backward, waiting for a scolding that never came. *What had I done?*

I began to realize this buzzing only happened when I was close to other people, and that somehow I could understand the thoughts of others. If I changed the way that I listened with my mind, other thoughts would cover my own—like radio interference. And so I could hear their thoughts, as if they were speaking them aloud.

Once I began to master it, the buzzing turned into beautifully complex patterns. It wasn't that I *could* listen to it; it was that I *had to* listen to it. I knew my friends' desires, fears, and secrets. I reveled in my own hidden knowledge—my own perfect secret. That is, until, when I was thirteen, I was kissed by Travis Jones.

I let him because I thought he liked me. But when he kissed me, his first thought was gross. His second thought was that he had won the bet and couldn't wait to post the picture on the Internet. *The picture?*

I smashed Travis's phone against the wall, then kicked him in his disgusting crotch. He screamed for help, but I didn't care. He still didn't feel as hurt as I did. I couldn't tell people why I had kicked him, so I said nothing. Mr. Robbson gave me a full week of detention. Every time he talked to me, his kind and gentle voice was betrayed by the unspoken thought that I was really just a mean kid, and that he was tired of parents who didn't teach their kids right from wrong.

That's when I started to be afraid of myself, ashamed of what I could do. I realized that I could only hurt people and they could only hurt me. I started to withdraw from others and keep to myself. I told my friends that they were rude and ugly, hoping that they would leave me alone. It worked, and they did. After that, nobody liked me.

In high school, people laughed about me and called me hurtful names. They left me notes in my desk saying that I was a loser, and sang songs about me in the hallways. I would rush past, trying to avoid hearing them thinking about me. Wondering why I acted so strangely. Thinking of the rumors they had heard—that even my mother didn't love me.

But they were wrong. My mother did love me. And somewhere on the other side of town, she still does. Just like I love her. But she has her own problems, her own worries. We all do.

I tried, once, to ask my mother if there was something differ-ent about me. I couldn't say it outright, so I said it another way. "Sometimes, I don't feel the same as other people. I think that I hear things they do not," I stated simply, and then waited.

No, not Nadine, she thought. *God, no. What have I done?* She bit her lip, her eyes wide. We stared at each other a long moment before she answered. I could hear her debating whether she should say anything, whether this was all a misunderstanding. *It can't be.*

"Our family is . . . different. A terrible curse. Something normal people don't talk about." Her eyes flicked back and forth as if checking that we were truly alone. "My uncle, he was afflicted. He told me not to . . . well, he heard things. Things that other people did not."

She stopped speaking, and stared at the closed blinds over my bedroom window. Tears streamed down her face. This silence, it hurt me the most. I loved my mother more than anything. She worked so hard, all day and sometimes into the evening, and her face always had a weary look to it. My mother's thoughts were always the hardest to read. They were muddled and confused. Trying to listen to her was like walking into a small rainstorm of love and fear, and fighting a strange wind of resistance, almost as if she were trying not to think at all.

But I could catch pieces of her thoughts anyway. Her uncle had been like me. He was dead now, they all were. All five of the circles, she thought. *Dead.* He had told her she was safe and that they didn't know about her, but warned her that she carried the condition, warned her not to have children.

A wave of cold washed over me, and for the first time in my life it felt inappropriate to listen like this. I grew afraid. There were so many questions. Who was dead? What did it mean to be like me? Why was my mother so scared? Why couldn't she just tell me?

I placed my hand over hers. "What was it called, what your uncle was? How he could hear—does it have . . . a name?"

She paused. I could hear her inner conflict, thinking that I probably needed to know since I would someday face the same choices that she did. I listened intently, knowing in my heart if she told me anything, this would be the only time. "Wavescanner. They call it wavescanning. It is . . . The Listener." I heard her thinking, again, of the five circles, that they were dead. No, that they *should* be dead.

Her cheeks flushed with shame. She was thinking that she had said too much, that she had promised not to speak of it, and that she had betrayed that promise. I could hear her resolve that she wouldn't speak of it again. That she must control herself, for my sake. She looked at me with panic. "And, please, never tell anyone. Of any of this. Can you promise me?"

"I promise," I answered. Her face washed with relief.

Her last thought before turning out the light was clear. She loved me, but she was afraid. Terrified. She wondered what she had done by allowing me to be born. "Nadi," she whispered, "We are carriers. These things you hear, it could be that they will pass." But her thoughts betrayed her.

She knows, I thought. *She knows my secret.* And it terrified her.

I, too, was a Wavescanner.

And that was when I started to understand why my mom was right: that being a Wavescanner, whatever that meant, was a curse. I understood why she was afraid, distant. Why she guarded her thoughts around me. I welled with sympathy and swore to protect my mother from me, from what I could do.

It was not long after that Mrs. Luzan, the school counselor, called my mom to her office. "Nadine has a severe learning disorder," she began. My mother sat silently, her face placid. Mrs. Luzan explained that I had an auditory processing disorder, with possible impacts to my executive function. I could not process sounds correctly, she said, and this led to challenges completing tasks, and interacting with others. She showed us pamphlets that stated how common this was, yet insisted that my condition was severe.

She told my mom that I would be placed into special classes. Mrs. Luzan turned to me. "Nadine," she began slowly. "I am very proud of your willingness to take this step." She smiled, and I nodded back, confused. My mother said very little, and Mrs. Luzan thought to herself that she wasn't a very caring mother. It hurt to hear this, and I wanted nothing more than to be away from her. So I decided I would attend the special classes, and say nothing of it.

But the classes weren't special at all. They were awful, and taught by a bored woman who only thought about her neighbor, and not in ways that would be decent to repeat. I gave up entirely.

I do think Mrs. Luzan tried to help me sometimes. But she sat too close to me as she praised my hard work, and I couldn't avoid her thoughts. She thought about science, her textbooks, and about diagnosing "the neglected child," as she called me. I decided she didn't care about the real me at all, so I didn't care about her back. And, eventually, she gave up on me too. In a way, this was a relief, as it was when they finally let me leave school for good.

Cars whizzed back and forth on the road ahead of me as I approached the home improvement store. Reaching the entrance, the large doors slid wide open with an overstated *whoosh*. I took a deep breath as I slipped inside.

It was like a zoo, only one full of people, running around with obnoxious abandon. A toddler zipped in front of me, thinking about how he would convince his dad to buy him chocolate at the checkout. Kids are always the easiest to scan. Adult thoughts can be complicated and hard to decipher, especially when someone is particularly conflicted or in denial. But not kids; they are easy. He wanted chocolate.

Thoughts bombarded me from all directions, and I felt sick inside. I needed to leave as soon as I could. Toilet parts. Where would they be? Massive walls of tools loomed to my right, and I could see towering stacks of lumber ahead, the smell of sawdust wafting my way. So I turned left.

A teenager in an oversized vest appeared in front of me, one hand on the rolling stepladder to his side. "Can I help you find something?" he said in a chipper voice. I could hear him hoping I would say no, because he was close to his break.

"No, thanks," I said, leaving him to continue stocking the cans of paint.

I sighed in relief. There they were: toilet parts. I grabbed the one I needed and started to leave. But halfway down the lamp aisle, I was caught by an unexpected thought. "I love you."

But who would feel love in a hardware store?

A young man stepped off of a footstool. He was tall, with

short sandy hair and a widening grin. Next to him, a young lady was short and just a touch overweight. Her hair was pulled up into at least a hundred tight braids, held on top of her head with a vibrant red cloth. Her eyes glittered gleefully in the array of artificial lighting. Neither wore the large vest that would have marked them as employees. I glared down at the footstool. They aren't supposed to leave those out for shoppers to use. Even I knew that; someone could get hurt.

I started to turn away, but then felt compelled to stay and watch, for just a moment. Then I realized why: neither one of them had noticed me. And neither one was thinking about me at all.

It was a lovely feeling.

Even without my abilities, I am a large woman, and used to being noticed. Yet, so used to avoiding people, not wanting to hear their mean thoughts, I couldn't actually remember the last time I'd watched people interact. I wondered if it was as awful as I remembered.

The young woman was holding a box depicting a lamp shaped like an orange foam finger. The sample sat on the shelf next to her, pointing enthusiastically toward the lofty ceiling. As lamps go, it was really ugly. "Thanks." She grinned. "Couldn't reach it, and was dreading having to call the ladder guy."

He chuckled. "I hate that guy," he said, laughing.

"Whoa, that's intense." She rested her free hand awkwardly on the shelf, and then let it fall back to her side.

"Oh, what?" the man replied. "No, I don't hate him, I was just—" He gaped at her blankly, looking ridiculous.

"I'm Joy." She shifted her weight, moving the lamp to her other arm.

"Yeah," the man responded. She raised her eyebrows at him. "I mean, oh, nice to meet you. I'm Ted."

I expected Joy to be thinking about Ted's overt lack of cognition, but instead, she was thinking that he was *cute*. I looked at him skeptically. His hair stuck out at odd angles, and he still had one foot up on the little black footstool. The wheels moved from under him, and he grabbed at the shelf to keep from falling.

"So, what's with the foam-finger light?" Ted offered.

"I thought it was funny." Joy held the box up slightly, before lowering it again.

"It is funny," Ted said, grinning. "It's number one, right?" He paused, and Joy did not respond. Fumbling over his words, he continued. "What are you going to do with it?"

"Oh, my dad has a TV room in the basement. We watch baseball games down there with our friends. I thought this would make him laugh."

"It will!" Ted smiled.

"Um, you know my dad?" Joy tilted her head, and finally started wondering if Ted was a little off or not.

About time, I thought.

"No, I mean, of course I don't know your dad. But I love baseball, and that lamp is awesome."

Ted was telling the truth about the baseball. But not about the lamp. He thought it was stupid and was wondering how long her poor dad was going to have to pretend that he liked it until it was "accidentally" broken while cleaning.

I grinned, in spite of myself.

Joy's thoughts were confused. She thanked Ted again for his help and started to walk away. Unlike Joy, Ted's thoughts were strong and clear. He was deciding whether to call after her, to ask for her cell number. But he didn't. As she turned the corner, I heard only one more thought. *I will never see her again. I should have said something.*

Ted started to meander away, toward the exit. Without really thinking about it, I snuck into the next aisle. It was full of extension cords, outlet hardware, and other electrical accessories. Joy stood silently, staring at a series of bins, each filled with international adapters. I didn't imagine that she needed them.

I approached her cautiously. She was scolding herself for walking away. I became angry. Why couldn't others hear thoughts, the way I could? All these stupid misunderstandings could be avoided if people just *listened*.

And now, these two people were walking away from each other when each was only thinking about seeing the other again. But they would never meet; I knew it. I felt overwhelmed by frustration, and I forgot this was none of my business. I forgot that I was just the loner from the top story of the West Side Apartments. I forgot everything except fixing things.

"Planning to travel?" I asked, looking at the array of adaptors.

Joy looked at me suspiciously. "Huh? Oh, no, sorry, was just thinking." She stepped to the side, assuming she was in my way.

"Um, no, I don't need adaptors either," I started. Her face grew even more distrustful, so I cut to it. "The guy back there called out as you were leaving. He said he loves baseball, and offered to . . . make nachos if you ever need them at your baseball party. Wasn't sure you heard."

Joy blushed, and bit her lip. "Oh, ok. I guess I didn't hear him. Thanks."

She moved her foot slowly in front of herself several times, before bounding back into the lamp aisle. I leaned up against a giant wheel of yellow cable, hoping to hear.

"Um, hey. Ted, right?"

"Oh. Um, yeah?" I could hear Ted walking back.

"I'm sorry I didn't answer you. Got distracted I guess." There was a pause. "You know, by the lamp." Another pause. "But yeah, we're having a playoff party next week. You should go. Here, give me your hand; I'll write my email." There was a short pause, and I could hear Joy trying to remember her email address. "Oh, and don't forget to bring your famous nachos."

"Of course not! Nacho master, here."

I winced. I forgot I had added that. Oh, well. If Ted couldn't figure out nachos, he didn't deserve the invitation. And besides, I hadn't said they were famous.

I walked back to the front, and tried to stay calm as the checkout lady scanned the replacement part. She was worrying about her husband, who was very ill. She wished she were at home. I felt a pang of sympathy for the woman. I hoped her husband wasn't as sick as she thought he was.

At this point, I didn't even know what I was doing, but I pulled a worn book out of my backpack. And then grabbed a chocolate bar from behind me and put it onto the counter. "Uh, ma'am?" She glanced sideways at me as she ran the chocolate over the scanner. It beeped. I handed her a ten dollar bill.

"Yes?"

"Well, there's a little boy in the store wearing a green striped sweatshirt. Can you give him this? If his dad says it's ok?"

"Sure," the lady shrugged. Her nametag said Judy.

"Judy, I'd also like you to have this. It's one of my favorites, and it makes me feel better when I'm worried."

She looked down skeptically at the book, adorned with a big golden dragon spread majestically across the cover. "Dragons? I don't know. And how do you know that—" Judy squinted, looking up at me suspiciously, before thinking, *Was I acting worried?*

Realizing my mistake, I rushed out of the store clutching the plastic part, without my change. I walked home quickly, staring at the ground and trying to calm myself.

When I got back, I walked past the sign with the misshapen palm tree without giving it a glance. I bounded up the stairs and then locked my door as soon as I got inside. I made the repair without much trouble, threw away the broken part, and stared at my piles of books.

It was 12:50. I poured a glass of water, pulled my chair up to the table, and thought about what I had heard today. Somehow, the memory of their thoughts stuck in my mind like a beautiful postcard from an exotic place. I tried to put it out of my mind, but found it difficult.

When Ms. Dovzhenko-Petit arrived, I decided not to be rude to her. It just didn't feel as fun as it normally did, and I was tired. Instead, I tried something different. "Your sweater is very pretty, Ms. Dovzhenko-Petit."

"What? Oh. I've had this one a while." She looked down at a patch of sapphire blue peeking through her fall coat. "But thank you." She sat down as always in my dining chair, staring at me curiously. I waited to be interrogated about my dusty books, or my laundry habits. But instead, the room stayed silent. Some kids rode past on the street below. One had a squeaky brake. It was always the same one, too. I had no idea why he didn't fix it.

Ms. Dovzhenko-Petit sat silently at the table. I wondered if the lack of questions meant her visit would be shorter than normal. I hoped so. I was feeling exhausted and really just wanted to go lie down.

"You seem subdued today, Nadine."

For once, I looked into Ms. Dovzhenko-Petit's eyes. I had always seen her as my jailer, but she seemed to be looking at me with real concern. And she was not thinking about relocation. She was, well, wondering if I was ok.

Her thoughts surprised me, and I found myself responding. "I've been thinking," I began, "that maybe I should get outside more. You know, talk to some people."

She nodded slowly. "That would be nice. I think you would enjoy it."

I nodded back, and hoped the conversation was over. Ms. Dovzhenko-Petit seemed to understand. Then she wondered if I would call my mother also. I grimaced. That wasn't her business. But it was a thought.

"Well, I will just use the restroom, then I'll be on my way." She stood up, clutching her purple leather purse, and stepped toward the small bathroom.

"The toilet flushes," I blurted.

"Yes, Nadine, it does." Ms. Dovzhenko-Petit smiled politely, and returned to remembering that I was irremediably crazy.

But that's ok. For a moment, she didn't.

Ϯime of the Spire

If you want no spoilers to *Spireseeker*, you should stop this story here.

This is the oldest story in the collection, and it addresses my Mom B's concern that I had killed all the unicorns in *Spireseeker*. (Yeah, sorry about that.) I'm not going to rehash the history here, but it was an odd time for me with a lot of trauma and depression and many other issues, and while it wasn't my going-in plan to feature "unicorn genocide" as a plot element, it happened. In my own mind, I'd always held hope that they survived—or perhaps I developed this in months to follow, as I wrote this piece in 2014 to tell the story of the wholly-murdered unicorns, for anyone who preferred this canon. (Several readers believe their death was a metaphor and that works too.) I sent it to several friends, asking if I should release it. They all responded: no. And one more politely: "Perhaps best to keep this one on the shelf." Well, guess what. The unicorns are back.

Content note for unicorn death, fire and burns, and a few simplistically graphic moments of violence.

Ιη the years since Aegra's death, I have not yet traveled to see the ruins of the Sanctuary. Part of my reasoning was the immense sadness that I felt at the loss of my friends, the unicorns.

Kick has always hoped they survived, but it has always been my belief that they did not. Ironwood was so certain that he would die, and Ironwood was a creature of great insight. And humans, like Kick, have such a capacity for optimism.

However, I recently had a strange dream, which I have recorded here. When a unicorn dreams, the dream will always come to be. But I am an elf, and the same thing cannot be said of my dreams.

I am still certain the unicorns did not survive Aegra's attack. The dream was likely a fancy of my own imagination, but—even so—perhaps a trip to the Sanctuary is finally in order.

- Beryl Spireseeker, Protector ex Unicornis

"The time of the Spire will end."

The phrase circled in Dorohoof's thoughts as she stared fretfully into the towering trees. The Spire loomed behind her—a glimmering pillar of stone under which the unicorns had lived for thousands of years. But she faced away, unwilling to be reminded, unable to shake the gloom she felt at Ironwood's warning. He had told her his secret before leaving, a secret only known to two others: Ironwood himself, and his long-time friend, Streamrider.

Ironwood had told Dorohoof that he had dreamed.

Among most creatures, dreams were barely of note, the details forgotten by the mid-day. But when a unicorn dreams, it is believed that the dream—good or bad—will always come true. Just as Jarinney, the most senior unicorn prior to his recent death, had dreamed long ago that someday a daughter and protector would arrive. That they would be the only chance to save Fayen from the cruel enslaver that was close to destroying it.

Ironwood's dream had taken that message farther. The dream had been dark, vague, and when he awoke he did not remember all of its details. But one thing was clear: when the protector arrived, the one they called the daughter of the unicorns, then with great certainty, the time of the Spire would end. And, he had told Dorohoof, he was certain that he—and thus the others as well—would die.

It must have been difficult for Ironwood to know such a thing. It explained his demeanor, his moods. For as the other unicorns celebrated the arrival of Beryl Spireseeker and her human companion Kick, and rejoiced that their savior of Fayen had arrived, Ironwood knew that it meant the end of his own kind.

Lost in her thoughts, Dorohoof barely noticed when Arborlay brushed against her.

"Hey."

"Oh, hi, Arb."

She and Arborlay had been close friends for a long time. He was sometimes dismissed as a bit of a joker, but she knew him better than most. He was thoughtful, and insightful, and Dorohoof enjoyed his company immensely.

"You seem worried."

Dorohoof shifted uncomfortably to the side. Ironwood had asked her to keep the dream a secret, to let the other unicorns continue on, carefree. "If it is to be their final days, let them live those in joy, not in worry."

So Dorohoof couldn't tell him. She had promised Ironwood to tell no one. But, still, there was reason to worry. Reason for them all to worry, as Ironwood and Streamrider had left, accompanying the unicorn elf, and had not yet returned. It was dangerous out in the mountains these days. The Spire, or the Sanctuary as the elves called it, was probably the only safe place left in Fayen. "I'm just hoping Ironwood and Streamrider return safely." It was true after all; she worried about this also.

Arborlay glanced at her thoughtfully, his olive-colored horn glinting in the sunlight. "I think they did the right thing by going. I believe in Beryl. I believe that she will save Fayen. Anything we can do to protect her is worth the risk. I would have gone myself had they let me."

Dorohoof tossed her long purple mane before looking back at Arborlay, his face fixated on her with a silly grin.

"You are a good friend, Arb."

"Don't worry so much, ok? Things happen for a reason."

Dorohoof snorted. "That says nothing, you know. If there was no reason, nothing could happen."

Arborlay's eyes twinkled back. "Of course. That's why I say it. Anything meaningful, you probably already know. Anyway, I—"

Dorohoof turned to retort, but stopped suddenly, seeing something new in Arborlay's eyes. It took her a moment to place it, as it was an emotion she had not seen before. But, unmistakably, it was terror.

"No," Arborlay whispered. "No."

Dorohoof turned quickly. She saw a large band of animals, lumbering up the horizon. She sensed no fear, no concern. They were mostly primates, men as well as gorillas. Some smaller animals accompanied them at the sides. They were pulling large carts behind them, carrying some sort of large canisters. It was like nothing Dorohoof had seen before. Even the elves avoided the use of metal; always preferring to work in wood, and cloth. A man in front of the grim party wore a dingy robe. He smiled maliciously, and uttered a few words to his crew.

As the men reached for the canisters, Dorohoof saw him. A gray unicorn, bound with ropes. His white mane heavily stained with blood, nearly matching his grand rust-colored horn. He was her mentor, the one she had grown up admiring, had always looked up to. In that moment, Dorohoof realized that he was her hero. It was Ironwood.

Ironwood did not look at her, did not see her. She called his name, and for a split second he started to turn, rearing into the air. The man in the robe looked nervously at the suddenly active creature, and whispered a command.

It was over before Dorohoof could even yell. She saw a flash of light, a glint against the blade of a huge axe as it swung through the air. It swung without hesitation or mercy. Ironwood's head split cleanly from his body, which teetered and fell with a thud.

Dorohoof ignored Arborlay's shrieks behind her. She rushed to fight, to avenge her mentor. But a wall of flame erupted in front of her, blocking her path. The men roared behind the flames.

In her shock, Dorohoof could neither move nor run. But then, it was as if Ironwood himself was speaking to her. It suddenly became clear, why he had told her. Why someone needed to know.

The secret keeper. Colorhusk.

But why her? Why hadn't he told him directly? There was not time to consider it. She turned to Arborlay, his face frozen and eyes wide. "Arborlay! We must find Colorhusk. I'll take left, you take right." Dorohoof forced herself not to look back toward the flames as both unicorns rushed off into the clearing.

Everyone knew that Colorhusk was named secret keeper by Jarinney several years ago. Jarinney had said he was too old and too weak to carry out the duties as required. Nobody knew, of course, what those duties were. If the duties were a secret, if they were not meant to know, then nobody asked.

But whatever it was that a secret keeper knows, she was certain now was the time they needed it. She raced ahead, as flames continued to burst into towering infernos—first behind, then to her side, then ahead. She choked on the thick smoke pooling around her.

"Ivyrun! Have you seen Colorhusk?" A small unicorn stood hiding behind a tree, shaking with fear. He stared at Dorohoof blankly. Dorohoof tapped her nose against him. He looked up, as though surprised. Words sprung out of him, though the look in his eyes did not subside. "The Meadow?" The young unicorn blinked quickly. "I don't know, those guys normally play in the meadow when it's nice like this."

Dorohoof wasn't sure who "they" were or whether it was even true. But the flames were growing taller. She nudged the terrified unicorn harshly. "Go, run away from the flames." The unicorn darted off.

Dorohoof galloped toward the meadow, her legs aching. As she reached its edges, she saw a group of at least a dozen unicorns running toward her. "Colorhusk! Colorhusk!" A large unicorn stepped forward, his mane a deep brown, and his body orange. She noticed his horn, a muted off-white, almost like the parchment the elves used, or the color of snow in the sunset. He was a magnificent unicorn, and Dorohoof wondered why she hadn't really looked at him before. She called again, "Colorhusk, we are being attacked. What is the secret?"

Colorhusk gazed over her shoulder, confused. She turned around, and saw dark smoke beginning to rise from the treetops. There was no time. She rushed into her words, "Creatures have arrived, led by men. Aegra's men. They killed Ironwood, and are burning the entire Spire with large bursts of flame. I thought, well, the secret keeper—"

Colorhusk's eyes narrowed, and Dorohoof realized what an extraordinary thing she had said. No unicorn had ever been murdered before. It was not such an easy thing to do, as unicorns could heal their own wounds. But Ironwood's death was swift, and something about him had been off. He did not fight back, he did not seem to resist. Those men had affected him somehow, she was sure of it.

A split second later, they were all racing toward the Spire itself, still towering into the sky as black smoke grew in spiraling towers around it.

As they approached the base of the Spire, unicorns were rushing around frantically, unsure of which way to run. "Here!" Colorhusk yelled. "The time of the Spire has arrived! Only now does it make sense." He rushed to a corner of the Spire, and began frantically tearing at the brush with his teeth. Others joined him, and soon a muddy layer of rock was visible.

Dorohoof glanced ahead, confused. *What could this do? It is mud and stone. There is no secret in that.*

Colorhusk reared into the air, and with great force, fell down upon the wall. Pieces of the mud began to chip away. "Help me! Help break this mud! There is an entrance!"

Dorohoof did not pause to consider the enormity of this statement, but rushed to assist. Her eyes burned with heat and smoke, but she and others kicked away at the mud, slowly revealing a hole in the side of the Spire itself. "Go!" Colorhusk yelled over the din. "Everyone, into the Spire."

One by one, a line of stunned and frightened unicorns ducked their heads, before walking into the small entrance they had created in the side of the Spire. Each unicorn's body tilted downward as they entered. "Keep going! I will be back."

Colorhusk raced back, nearly running into the flames. Dorohoof gasped, but immediately understood. She hurried after him, then as he ran back toward the mountainside, she turned the other way, toward the lake.

Dorohoof raced through the trees, urging anyone she found to return to the Spire. "You will be safe, you must go!" she urged a group of frightened friends. As she ran further, she heard whimpering ahead of her. A young unicorn had fallen onto the ground, and a tree trunk sat firmly over her legs. Her mane was singed, and burns spread across her back. Dorohoof winced. She pushed the tree off to the side, and her voice hoarse, she wheezed, "You've got to heal yourself."

"I can't. I'm too scared. My legs are broken. I'm ... I'm dying." Dorohoof looked down at the little unicorn, her face and horn coated with mud. She looked familiar. "What is your name?"

"Snowylight," the unicorn whimpered.

The flames drew closer around them. "Come on, Snowylight, you've got to try. Who are your parents?"

The question distracted the girl. "Mountainmark and Runnerwind," she whispered. Dorohoof paused. She did not know them well, but knew she could not face them again, not without their little filly. "Think of them, then. Close your mind and think of only your parents. Think of being better so we can run to them."

The unicorn closed her eyes. Dorohoof watched the flames

draw near. She didn't want to rush her, but knew they would both die if they didn't move soon. The heat was nearly unbearable, the smoke suffocating. Dorohoof could stave off burns for a bit, but she could not heal herself if she lost consciousness. She stared at Snowylight.

"Heal yourself. *Now!*" It was her own mother's tone of voice, and it seemed silly to use it under these circumstances but it was all she could think to do.

Snowylight's eyes closed tightly, before she sprung up, her burns suddenly gone, her legs mended. Dorohoof urged her to follow, and they broke off again through the woods. "Go, that way, toward the Spire! Your parents will be looking for you— find them and go to the Spire itself. You will be safe there; you'll see."

Snowylight looked gratefully at her, and paused. "Go!" Dorohoof urged. "We will speak later!"

Snowylight galloped off, and Dorohoof could spare her no more thought, as the flames were again licking at her legs. She ran through all of the common gathering areas on the side of the Spire facing the lake, hoping Colorhusk would cover the rest, the direction he had run.

A few unicorns were hiding under a rock overhang, she urged them to return to the Spire. The goallog fields were empty, so she ran ahead. As she turned back into the thick trees, she jumped out of the way of a white burst of flame. Just then, she heard a crack, and before she could again move a burning limb was across her chest, pinning her to the ground.

She concentrated. She was not going to give up, not now. She strained, and pushed, but the tree would not move. Her chest tensed, her heart beating quickly. She thought of her own mother, probably ushered into the Spire by now, worrying about her. She thought about funny, caring Arborlay, and then a new thought came into her mind—of Colorhusk, so bravely rushing into the forest to ensure every last unicorn was safe. She shook her head. She had to get out of here.

But it was no use, the limb had her pinned. She refused to panic. Something to pull with her teeth, then? Something to break loose? She looked around, but had to close her eyes as the ash was stinging them beyond her ability to tolerate it. She let out a loud cry, furious at herself to be stuck this way. Suddenly the limb lifted into the air. Colorhusk stood above her, looking down at her with a worried expression. "Are you ok?"

"Yeah, sure. But let's get out of here." Dorohoof stood up, and concentrated. She had done this before, usually after declaring house rules on a rough game of goallog. With a quick push, her burns healed, as did her broken ribs. She gasped, not having even realized any bones were broken. Relief spread across Colorhusk's face as she stood.

Then she saw it. Another branch, flaming with orange and yellow spirals was flying directly at Colorhusk's head. There was no time, even to warn. She jumped at Colorhusk, her hooves extended in front of her, knocking him roughly away. She glanced at a wide stain of red blood as his side scraped against an outcrop of rough gray rock. The branch flew past him.

Colorhusk's eyes were closed as he healed his wounds. Dorohoof stared at him with concern as they got to their feet again. "Even?" he asked.

"Even." She almost thought that he smiled, but dismissed it as the fire again began to envelop them. Who would smile at such a time, anyway? "Do you think we found everyone?"

"I think so. I made it around that way, you came from there?" He pointed with his horn, indicating the lake. "That should catch the normal places, outside of the Spire clearing itself." "There might be someone left. We can't be sure."

Colorhusk stamped a hoof. "I know, but we can't risk it. We stay out here any longer, we're dead for certain. Can't help anyone then." As if to illustrate the point, both unicorns leapt out of the way of a mass of stone crumbling down the side of the hill. "Besides, we can't see through this to find anyone else. We've done all that we can."

Dorohoof grimaced. She looked over at Colorhusk and felt a strange spark within her. She wanted to live. No, she needed to live. He was right. "Let's go."

The unicorns again ran, leaping over the flaming limbs and falling rock. They could barely see any longer, the smoke was so thick. Even without their vision, it was as if they instinctively knew how to return to the Spire. It drew them forward. Dorohoof concentrated, trying to heal her burns as she ran, but she was not experienced at it, so instead she focused only on moving as quickly as she could, and avoiding any further hazards. She cringed, seeing Colorhusk's singed, flaking skin. *Do I look like that too?*

"Come on, we're almost there." She could barely make out his voice, raspy and cracking. Her eyes burned, her limbs numb.

She tripped more than once, and Colorhusk urged her on. Finally, though she saw nothing around her, he whispered, "Debris. Pile it here." He pulled her through some sort of rock, and she began to pick up small pieces of debris and pile them where he directed. Everything was hot, searing her lips as she worked.

Down a sort of ramp they walked, and she could no longer hear, or feel. Her limbs gave way, and she lay down onto a cold slab of rough stone. Then she remembered it, that spark. The need to survive. She reached into herself, and pushed as hard as she could. Then everything went black.

When she came to, she could hear the echoes of voices, and hooves upon the stone floor. She opened her eyes, but it was dark and she could barely make out shadows around her. Colorhusk stood next to her, wobbling on his feet. Runnerwind stood next to them both, with a rolled bark, full of water. "Here, drink this."

Dorohoof drank the water gratefully. *Runnerwind.* "Snowylight?"

There was a murmur around her. "She is here, she is fine. We are all here. Only two are missing."

"Streamrider and Ironwood?"

In the dim light, she could see the unicorn nod.

"They will not return." The cave grew silent. "I saw Ironwood die. And Streamrider would not have left him."

Dorohoof looked around. Her eyes were adjusting to the lack of light. "Everyone else is here?"

"They are," Runnerwind responded. "Thank you for saving Snowylight. I cannot tell you—" The unicorn could not continue.

"How long have we been here?" Dorohoof squinted.

"Without the sun, it is hard to say, but I think a full day now. There is little light, but ample supplies. There is a small stream that runs through the rock, and curved bark to make what tools we might need. There are several rooms, all interconnected. Further back, there is even thin soil, where small edible roots grow."

Dorohoof paused. "Colorhusk, who made this place?"

"I don't know. When the role of secret keeper was passed to me, I was simply told there was an entrance into the Spire itself. I was told where it was, to tell no one of its existence, and only to break its seal in a time of greatest need. This seemed to qualify."

After what seemed like a couple of days, the unicorns grew tired of the dark. Colorhusk went back up the ramp and broke through the makeshift wall that he and Dorohoof had made. When he returned, he was grim.

"There is no sign of the attackers. They destroyed everything they found, and then left. The air is still smoky, the land barren, and the trees charred beyond any ability to recover. We cannot stay here, not for several more years until the land begins to heal. If that ever happens." Colorhusk paused.

Dorohoof sensed his hesitation. There was more. "The village?" She knew he would have checked; he was gone long enough.

"Destroyed. Some bodies cover the paths, many others are burned to ash. Only a few partial dwellings stand. None survived. There is no evidence of any survivors. I wish we could have helped, but we never would have made it, even if we had tried. And there was no shelter, no—" Colorhusk could not finish. His ears pulled back, and he closed his eyes.

Only silence followed. Dorohoof bowed her head. "It is not our fault, what happened. You are right, we never could have made it to the village alive."

Mountainmark stepped up behind Runnerwind and whispered, "What should we do?"

Dorohoof peered at Colorhusk, his eyes still closed. But she knew the answer. "We should go there first. Burn the remaining dead. It is what they would do."

There was no joy stepping out into the sunlight again, only a dull feeling of warmth. The unicorns did not gallop, but walked at a slow, deliberate pace down the hill toward the elven village. When they reached it, they walked through each home, dragging any remaining bodies, even limbs, or fragments of robes, out into where the ceremonial garden had been.

The garden had once been full of life, color, and fragrance. It was an empty space now, black and void. They struck a blaze, and most closed their eyes as what was left of the protectors vanished back into the dead soil of their former Sanctuary.

The younger unicorns turned away, the older stared sadly. There were no words spoken, no goodbyes. Only a sense that the elves would have appreciated this small tribute.

Dorohoof approached Colorhusk quietly. "We should leave now, before dark. I don't think we should spend even a night here like this, and nobody will want to return to the cave. Not after seeing the sun again."

Colorhusk nodded. "Friends. I will be leaving for the forest, higher in the mountains, to find stones and moss these wicked flames have not touched. If you choose to follow me, you are welcome. If you wish to find your own path, it is your choice. Either way, I am certain we will meet again."

Several of the unicorns left immediately at his words, walking off with their families beside them. Dorohoof stood with Colorhusk. She could see her parents standing to the side, nuzzling against each other, but not leaving. Snowylight approached her, and stood still.

Dorohoof looked down at Snowylight. "What is that?" It was an abrupt way to ask, but she was tired and sad, and had little room for eloquence.

"A ribbon. From the girl's suit." Dorohoof leaned closer. A silky ribbon hung from Snowylight's mouth, untouched by fire or ash. By the girl, it was clear who she meant. Kick, the human girl that had accompanied Beryl, the unicorn elf, to the Spire. They were the ones rumored to be part of Jarinney's dream, the only ones with a chance to save Fayen.

Snowylight asked her, "Can you attach it?" Dorohoof took the ribbon in her teeth, and pulled it through Snowylight's damaged mane before looping the ends together. Snowylight smiled. Perhaps it was that smile, but Dorohoof felt a new sense of purpose. She turned to the others, and stood tall. "This ribbon survived. Something tells me the human does as well. She will save Fayen. Kick—and Beryl Spireseeker together. I have not dreamed it, but I know it just the same.

"Now, let Colorhusk lead us. Today, our friends have died." She nodded both to the smoldering grave of the elves, and also to the garden itself. "But we are still here, and tomorrow is another day. We know that not every elf was here; perhaps a few still survive. The lowlands are dry and harsh, no longer suitable for our kind. Let us return to the forest, as we were before the time even the Elders remembered, before the elven village was formed.

"If someday the elves return to the mountains to find us, maybe one day we will again roam together as companions, and soulmates. And if not, then we will live our days in peace, in the natural sanctuary that has always been ours to share.

"Tomorrow is another day. The time of the Spire has ended, but the days of the unicorn have not."

Colorhusk stood closer to Dorohoof, nuzzling the side of her face. Dorohoof stepped back, surprised, and Colorhusk smiled. "How could the days of the unicorn ever end, Dorohoof? Unicorns never say goodbye."

At that, Colorhusk took off into a gallop, the others following behind. And they did not stop until the trees were again green, and the ground again soft. As the sun set over the mountains, it revealed a rich blanket of stars that assured the unicorns a peaceful night of sleep, and the promise that the sun, as well as Fayen, would rise again.

VH

The next two stories represent another attempt at Mad Scientist Journal in late 2019, in this case not an anthology, but their final (Winter 2020) issue of the actual *Mad Scientist Journal*. I had just been out at Hector & Jimmy's with my parents, and it came up how their (and my childhood) garage has a glorious spray-painted Van Halen logo inside of a closet. My dad said: "You could make a short story out of that." I couldn't get it out of my mind (like the mystical VH itself) and so with the deadline for the MSJ last issue approaching, I gave in and wrote it up. In fact, for historical details, I got both my parents to answer some questions (though I never sent them the story itself). So this piece, despite being ridiculous, is pretty special to me. And, even though this story didn't make it in, I did get a short, funny, classified ad into the final issue and I was pretty excited about that.

I almost rewrote this piece into 3rd person for this collection, because I wanted it that way initially and felt it would be stronger, but MSJ requires 1st person, with a specific narrator, as we've discussed. However, when I started to do so, it felt wrong, because it would get me back into editing and that's not what this collection is. So if anyone wants to publish a 3rd person retelling of VH, or like work with Van Halen (late edit: his estate) on a movie deal or maybe turn this into, like, a Bill and Ted 4, you know, call me. And either way, enjoy the obviously best line of the collection, featured in this piece, with a backstory about a specific person that I've never got to say it to.

RIP Eddie Van Halen, 1955-2020

A true story by Laura Matthews

"DAMN it," I muttered, as the curly cord, stretched beyond its last gasping breath, gave way and pulled the phone into flight. As I lunged back into the room, hoping to at least catch the base before any of the little plastic plugs snapped off, I tripped over the floormat from last week's garage-sale and fell inelegantly against the small table, watching in slow motion as the houseplant that Mom insisted I couldn't kill spun onto the floor, covering the yellowed linoleum in loose potting dirt.

"So I guess I'll call you back," I grumbled into the disconnected receiver before tossing it back onto the side chair's plaid cushion. Turned out, Dick from church had been by earlier in the week to borrow the new Electrolux Special Edition in exchange for a guilt trip about his ailing grandfather, so now I just stood there and stared at the dirt like maybe it would just leave.

It didn't. After about two seconds imagining scooping the weird looking dirt with my hands—even as an actual scientist, I never wanted to know what those white balls were—I remembered that tiny broom closet in the basement. The one they'd forgotten to empty.

I'd bought the house just around Thanksgiving, right as everyone told me I'd never find a house in the winter. Certainly, the one thing people didn't need in the snow was a house. Or maybe everyone else planned out their lives better than I had and knew when house-buying was appropriate and not.

The woman I'd bought it from had been just as eager to sell it as she'd been to find it, it seemed. A single mom with a teenage son, she'd not sounded eager to tell all the details. Some "need to get back to Minnesota" was all I got from it, but that was just fine. I had my own issues, and wasn't in the mood for a "working woman" connection.

Right now, those issues included a kitchen nook covered in underwatered potting soil and a mother who probably thought I'd hung up on her. I kept expecting the phone to ring again, but I was pretty sure I'd killed it. I wasn't buying another one of those cords. When I went down for the broom, I decided, I'd grab that electrical tape too.

I'd tried to do the right thing about the brooms, or whatever was in there. After the moving guys told me about them, I'd sent the house's seller a note—her new address was written on the paperwork whether it was supposed to be or not—and said the usual things. Thanks for selling me your house. It was lovely to meet your son. (I don't think I even met him, but I saw him in the parking lot at the agent's office.) Oh, I then mentioned, you left some tools in the basement. Let me know if you want them.

It wasn't until I'd already licked the stamp that I remembered she was, by now, in Minnesota, and wasn't going to come back for a broom, or whatever else was in there. Free broom, then. Take that, Dick.

I'd sort of been avoiding the basement, to tell the truth. I didn't mind the musky smell; it was comforting and reminded me of Nanna's place. In fact, maybe it was because I liked it too much. Even in the winter's cold, it felt cozy, but without the artificial warmth of the groaning heater upstairs. It's almost like . . . it called to me, but that's creepy and you never knew when the lawyers were listening.

I walked down, my fingers gripping the worn handrail, and edged toward the back, where the rumored brooms awaited, at the end of the concrete wall where all the screens were leaned up. Sure enough, there was a little closet. Sort of. What I saw was a narrow sheet of brown-painted plywood with a ten-cent knob screwed into it. The way the concrete blocks bowed to the side, it was almost like they'd realized they'd made the basement crooked, so they'd hinged in this piece of plywood to cover up the shoddy construction. It didn't work.

Not that I actually cared what the back of the basement looked like.

I opened the door, and realized the plywood blocked the light from the hanging bulb, leaving the closet itself in the dark, like a tiny basement black hole. Sighing, I wandered back to my dad's old metal tool chest, that these days mostly held the huge flashlight I got on sale at the hardware store. It had "Super Flashlight" printed on the side, which I thought was pretty bold for a sale flashlight, so I had to have it. Thing's held up pretty well; I admit.

I turned Super Flashlight on, and walked back to the plywood door, which had swung back against the blocks. I flipped it open.

And stopped in place.

The back side of the door was painted. Gold spray paint, swished across the brown-painted "door" like chariot tracks of the gods. Why did I think that? It was spray paint.

I craned in to read it. There were horizontal lines on each side, and a swipe up and down, and then a crowded slanty *H*. As if, it were a stylized "V H"—then I recognized it. *Van Halen.* Right? That group with the teacher song. That group my exercise instructor played over and over again last spring in rhythm with that giant swinging rope until I quit because I'm not five.

Why would it be here? Why on the back of a door no one would pass through? Staring, my hand reached for a stringy old broom and I walked back up the stairs.

Ah, crap, I'd forgotten the tape. I leaned the broom against the snow shovel and headed back downstairs. Walking down again, I started to feel extra strange, like a premonition. Or a crush.

I was too old for this. And my kitchen was covered in dirt. And I half expected to see Mom's fully-loaded Oldsmobile rolling up at any moment.

But it didn't, and I got the kitchen as clean as I was going to until the next time I mopped. I'd just mopped yesterday, and no floor was going to get that level of attention from me. Turned out, the cord was solidly dead and not tapeable, so I guessed a trip to Sears was in order.

Thing was, I couldn't stop thinking about that closet. I get it: VH. Someone liked Van Halen. The teenage kid, I guess, as his mom was older than me and seemed more like the showtunes type. Anyway, Van Halen had that guy with the tiny glasses that hopped around. These kids needed better music. Not music videos. Not fancy special effects: who cared if they could show a guy four times on the same screen? *Music. Rock & Roll.* The real deal.

I remember when Elvis was first on Ed Sullivan. I was at Nanna's house. She turned off the TV and made us play Yahtzee. That's all you need. A star so bright your Nanna can't watch him. Glasses guy; what does he do? Whoop and howl?

I really needed to stop thinking about that closet and get back to work. Making a quick sandwich, I wiped off the knife and stared at the marked-up calendar hanging on the wall.

So it must have been the son that did it. What possessed him to paint inside of the closet? Was this his best rebellion against Mr. Mistoffelees? But why the back of a crappy basement door? There was no room in the closet; wouldn't hiding it somewhere in his room be more rebellious? This was ridiculous. I needed to get to Sears and buy a new phone.

The whole way there I was thinking about Van Halen kid. And the whole way back. I even turned on the Oldies' station in the car and it was Beatles' Weekend, and I remembered how Mom said they were ok until they got weird. Which was actually when they got good.

While I was at the mall, I picked up some of that new calcium cleaner and I was soaking the slow shower head like on the commercial, and the whole time I was thinking about Van Halen.

Giving up, I walked back downstairs.

Grabbing Super Flashlight like a sword, I shined it into the closet. There, the golden sparkle of VH beamed like a ray into heaven. But, I'd seen it already. What was I supposed to do?

The floor was filthy, but there was an old burlap deck chair cushion folded against the rakes and brooms that didn't look too awful, so I opened it up and sat down, leaning back to gaze up at the spray-painted tribute.

As the basement disappeared around me, I found myself in a dark garden, surrounded by twinkling stars and a soft scent of jasmine. A familiar guitar riff swirled around me, as Mick's sweet, deep vocals dove into "Paint It, Black."

I fought the sensation. This wasn't possible. My records were taped into a moving box labeled "records" and my 8-track player was broken, and the only things I had on tape were gifts from Mom and that Weird Al guy the lab techs couldn't stop talking about.

Paint It, Paint It . . .

When that song came out I listened to it constantly. Billy from Gym told everyone I was too ugly to kiss. My science teacher heard him say it, and tried to comfort me by telling the whole class that as smart as I was, I wouldn't need to worry about that. My friend, Marv, had just had his accident, and . . . there was more, too.

Mick kept singing. He sang about the door, and the cars, and the sea. The colors. The darkness.

I don't know how long I sat there, my eyes closed. Jane said "Lady Jane" was about her and I never argued, and we listened to *Between the Buttons* over and over until her dad replaced the needle.

I used to go to Jane's house, because her mom let her buy *Satanic Majesties*, which sounded completely off-limits. We pretended it was the best music we'd ever heard, singing "She's a Rainbow" as loud as we could while her brother glared from across the room.

I was in college by the time "Sympathy for the Devil" was released, and I figured it was me, the way all the other scientists talked me down and called me honey. But I kept singing, I worked harder, and I got my degree.

Turning my head to the left, I saw the spray can there, the one he must have used. Should I add my mark? Leave a footprint in the snow?

The horizontal lines burst from the slanty VH like rays of the sun. Laughing, I stood and brushed the dirt from my jeans.

I'd better get that phone hooked up and call my mom.

Ms. Laura Matthews is busy making something of herself, at least she's determined to before she turns 35. Having just bought her own house, she is well on her way. She loves rock music, Mexican food, and she's given up pop for the winter. No one will ever be as good as the Stones, and she bets they will still be out there playing music ten years from now. Maybe for the rest of the century.

My Perfect Creation

Given my hunch that MSJ wouldn't go for the Van Halen story, I wanted to give them something full-on, all-in mad sciencey for their final consideration. They didn't go for this either, but I think it's pretty fun. Hope you enjoy! And, with the closure of this awesome publication, you will definitely not see as much 1st person from me. 3rd with strong POV is where I like to live. But for now, I hope you enjoy Dr. Numbers' telling.

Lab notes by Dr. Star Numbers

I have been working on this for years! Not only this; I've had lots of projects and have created many things. Some creations are objects that people can use, and others are designed to make a boom or a flash.

Last month, I opened a vial of swirling interdimensional smoke which did nothing but impress the townsfolk and this is fine because so much of being able to create is keeping one's self in view. One fly did fly into the brief interdimensional passage but as he could not fly into a world where he could not exist, and very few worlds hold people, and very many hold flies, I feel confident his last week on Earths will be magnificent.

Speaking of magnificent, I have been working on this creation for longer than my mind is quite able to recall in a linear sense but you would consider it very long, I am certain.

In all this, I have created the most perfect thing I could imagine. It is me, without being a mad scientist.

Wouldn't you like to see it? You without flaws. You without

questionable choices. You, that enjoys walnuts and thus can indulge in a raw foodist taco! The taco is not important but the choices have certainly been.

Kira was my friend, and Kira was not so mad, and Kira has a very lovely life now, with a partner and children and never does she worry that her creations are not enough and that her laboratory will not be paid, or that people are whispering behind her back that if only she did a thing that people cared about then her worries would be none.

I know that my creations have helped people, but as we are surrounded by science, it is not always so specifically known when the science has changed the footpath of your life forever, and so people wander on and say why would she do what she does?

She should be responsible. I've made a creation just that way. A responsible me. A me that was like Kira, and Kira's parents didn't worry about her playing with me and I heard she went to the beach this week!

One more condition: I programmed the DNA that she must also be happy. Perfect. And happy. The energy can only flow through conduits and I've misplaced nothing.

I have everything ready in my lab. The interdimensional hologram is fired, and the spectral looptonium acquired from places I cannot admit to you that I went, and I've shielded the building and put [NO SOLICITATIONS] on my door and I bribed the flies with interdimensional freedom and everything is *ready to go!*

Kira gave me my name. I said that I was too strange and she said I was a star, and I wanted to be that star. For her. For others who were sometimes sad and whom science could help.

Before I met her, I tried to hide, and after I met her, I knew who I was and I just lived that person and I trusted that the universal gravity put me here because this is where I need to be.

I think I was wrong. So here's my secret. I am going to meet me, the correct me, and if I have the looptonium condenser set up correctly—and I do—then we can trade and she can take my place and I can do it all over.

Every quantum needle is set, and the DNA extracted and modified, and I made a giant lever because if you remake yourself it must be with a giant lever, and I pull it.

Is it working? My heart almost stops. So many years I've worked at this. It must be working.

It must.

Vvrrrrrreeer.

Oh, that was a perfectly scientific sound. I circle the platform and see that she is building. A soft pink shirt, and sensible trousers that fit the way they were intended and her hair is cut just right. Her soft smile is not the one I see in the mirror and her eyes do not flicker.

She is me, but perfect.

"Hello," I whisper, not wanting to frighten her. Science excites me, of course, but I am not her, or at least not yet.

I expect her to ask where she is but she does not.

"Hello," she answers, her smile still as soft.

I almost make a mistake. I almost tell her who I am. That I love science and that my name is Dr. Star Numbers, and that I make creations, some that people like, and some that only I like and that I never have money or peace and peace is all I want but that clearly costs some money.

"Tell me about yourself?" I ask instead.

"I love reading books," she says.

That's nice.

"I've planted a lot of flowers."

I can't argue with flowers, but what I really want to know is—

"I work hard."

Now I'm sort of annoyed. What's that mean: work hard? I work all the time; I've worked all the time since I was little and my friend was sad and I said let's create something.

"What about you?" she asks, too polite to want to take the spotlight for long.

I can't tell her about me. It would ruin the creation. I can't tell her that people don't like me like they probably like her and I can't tell her that I'm going to swap with her, and we're going to start all over.

"What do you do? For work?" I stammer, with one moment of curiosity because this is my problem in the first place. Maybe she works hard at something great. Just something that also pays the bills. Maybe she's a powerful executive, or maybe she teaches children or cleans rooms.

"Whatever they tell me." She smiles and tilts her head.

I throw my body on the switch and she fizzles out of sight and I'm left alone again, with nothing, when I was supposed to be here, becoming my own perfect creation.

I hear a cry, outside. I'm not sure what it is but someone might need some help. A person, or a child. Maybe it's a little cat.

I'll come back to this later.

Dr. Star Numbers is a mad scientist with laser vision, like a thousand cats, and an obsession with Madonna. Her inventions are too many to name, and she wishes robots were more advanced because people can be a lot sometimes. Robots would get it, she thinks.

X

The next two were written for a flash fiction website in 2018. This first one was submitted and came back with a one-star editor's rating. A matter of taste? I hope you enjoy this absolutely five-star moment.

X was a molecule. She was a speck.

X swam among the other specks, invisible. X was not a speck. She was more.

X shouted into the sea of others, "I am someone."

X was someone. She stood tall and walked the corridors of a large building. The others passed her, and they did not listen when she spoke. "You will listen," she called. It echoed down the hallways and her voice felt small.

X spoke louder. She grew larger. She became the building, and then the sky above it. She spoke above them now, and no one heard her. "You must hear me," she cried. "I have things to say."

X became the stars. She spun with the galaxies. She saw the universe, gasping at its reentering boundaries. A horizon of awe beyond even her reach. Still, no one paid attention. They went about their day. "I am here, and I am speaking. I will never stop speaking." She shouted across the void.

And then X understood.

X returned, back into the body that held her. A body of trial, and yearning. A mind of ideas, opinions, and beliefs. And never again would X let anyone ignore her.

"I matter," she said. "And I will never stop speaking."

LORD OF THE DEMONS

This second piece was my actual favorite of the ones I wrote, but those involved didn't care for it, so I never submitted it. Well then, I now present to you, the totally awesome "Lord of the Demons".

THE Lord of the Demons should not be awakened!

The Lord of the Demons felt the fire in her throat. Stifled, under the heat of many layers. Beasts crawled on her legs, their claws pressing into her awakening flesh.

She reached for a foul cloth, to further bear the brunt of her infestation, borne of her youthful spawn. Creaking the beams beneath her, Lord of the Demons rose. She crept forward, prowling through her lair, owning the souls that crossed her path.

Stretching, she grew to new heights. Sounds played in the distance, of buffoonery and greed. Lies and destruction. Foretelling of the sweltering heat that would only continue to grow.

Creatures wrestled and fought, scrubbing the stones that they had left untended, denying their eternal burdens that she was not here to allay.

Banished, she expelled them from her lair, tossed into steel cages to journey to their judgment! Whether their deeds had been conducted; it was too late for her to determine.

With cubes of frosty ice, she laced the metal implement, draining the essence from the corpses of roasted beings and pouring their liquid fire over the ice. She added flax milk and maple syrup. That always made it better.

Taking a breath, she turned on the shower. And sipped the latte.

Today was going to be a great day.

ʀain's ᴄloud

For my first effort to get into big-name publications in January 2019, for some odd reason I wrote a wizard romance. I personally love this story. After it was not taken by two publications (I was told by one editor the stakes weren't high enough, but this story wasn't meant to be about those kind of stakes) I decided to save it for this collection, for my readers—who enjoy subtle. I really hope you like it.

WITH a pop, a spire of gray smoke whirred and fizzed into the air, scattering into a gray haze that hovered over the valley.

"That's it," Hana muttered, reaching for her walking stick and slinging her canvas bag over her shoulder.

It was common knowledge in the village that a wizard had moved into the old abandoned tower atop the overlook. Not needing any more hexes in their lives than they already had, they'd stayed away. Yet, over time, as the smoke flew from the tower with increasing frequency, people were losing their patience.

Sure, the dark smoke—or whatever that cloud was—didn't seem to harm anyone, in the sense that there was no smell, residue, or ash. Perhaps it was simply a wizard thing.

Yet, no one should have to look at a dark cloud.

Hana stopped a moment to rest. Her knees didn't hold together these days the way they used to, and she softly cursed the wizard for not living down on the river. With a sigh, she imagined herself sitting on a dock, her bare feet running through the rippling water.

Much of the morning had passed, and after a long turn through the forest, Hana was relieved to see a gap in the trees, showing she had not strayed deeper. Keeping her walking stick firmly in front, she walked toward the ledge, just until she could see the valley below.

She hadn't been up this way in a long time, but the view caught her breath, just for a moment. She gazed down at the little gathering of homes dotting the valley below. Looking up to scan across the early autumn sky, her eyes rested on the darkness wafting through the air, carrying a slight shimmer in its wake.

With a grunt, she turned back to follow the rough path, which started to congeal into an actual stone walkway, which then formed into a set of rough-hewn stone steps.

They ended at a narrow tower.

The tower was older even than the village; no one knew its age or origin. Its stone blocks were said to be deteriorated, but here, they stood as though they'd been placed a summer ago. Dark green vines wove and crossed together around elongated oval windows and accents of quartz-veined stone.

She knocked at the door.

"Hello," she called. "I'm from the village; I'd like to talk." The wizard was clearly here. Smoke rose from the spire as she stood in the tower's shadow, and everyone knew a wizard always attended their craft.

With a *creak*, the door grated open.

Hana walked inside, glancing around at the round, unfurnished room. Seeing that the stone path continued on in and through the door, rising into a spiral staircase, she stopped, folding her hands over the knob of her stick.

"Hello, I'd prefer not to walk into an enchanted tower on my own. If you're around, I'd appreciate you joining me here in the entrance. Thank you."

Starting to decide maybe she'd just let the village manager deal with this, she started to turn.

"Uh, wait," a voice said, thin and shaky. "Sorry, I'm here."

A figure descended the stairs, wearing a metallic-threaded blue robe that she couldn't help but think he'd thrown on moments before.

"Master Wizard Stormbringer?" The presence of a wizard spread quickly in any province. At this point, she'd heard every tale about Master Wizard Stormbringer from the one where he'd murdered his whole family to the one where he spent his days as a toad so he could peer into windows. She doubted any of them were true.

"Yes, that is I." He reached for something, seemed to realize that nothing was there, and then stood taller.

"Well, as I've said, I'm Hana from the village. I'm here to make a request." She raised a hand as he started to speak. "No, sorry, not a wizard request. Something more . . . neighborly."

He stood unmoving, and Hana wondered how often the wizard employed social activity. "Your . . . wizardry . . . is disturbing the village."

"The village?" His eyes flicked. "I've kept it all contained, haven't I?"

"I'm not sure what you've contained," Hana continued. "But your smoke pops and cracks in the middle of the night. And during the day, the smoke carries over us, creating an eerie black cloud."

"Pops and cracks?" He scrunched his nose, causing his beard to wriggle.

"Yes. It wakes the babies. Forget the babies," she amended, "it wakes me. And once I'm awake, it's done for the night."

"Rain," he said.

"No, smoke. Your black smoke." She pointed upward, as though through the tower itself.

"My name is Rain. It's not a wizarding name, but my mother liked it." He glanced away at the light which streamed against the empty stone wall. "She's long-passed now. Wizardry prolongs life. Even my sisters—" He shrugged.

Sadness settled into his eyes. "The Conclave didn't like it. Said it wasn't a good wizard name, and dubbed me Stormbringer. I don't like it."

Wouldn't be Hana's choice, but it was a powerful enough name. "Why not?" she asked, not meaning to be personal, but not finding the man so intimidating.

"Makes me sound scary," he said.

Their eyes met.

He glanced away. "Well, you've met the others, of course. Furorious, Shindrelf, Urlarian, Steve, Thunderbalst—"

"That is *not* his name," she murmured, not meaning to say it aloud.

"Steve? But it is. Yet, Rain wasn't good enough." He grimaced.

Hana stood there, shifting her weight against the hard stone floor. It wasn't so comfortable standing in an empty room, but maybe he'd agree to her request if she showed him she meant no harm. He had opened up about his name.

"So, Rain, what do you do here? I admit, I don't understand wizarding. Is it a . . . job?"

"A job?"

"Sure. In the village, some mend the fabrics, and others sew them. Some forge metals, or harvest crops." What she wanted to say was, *What does a wizard actually do?* but that didn't seem so polite.

"Oh, sure. Like that. I suppose you could call me retired." He ran a hand down his beard, twisting it in his fingers before letting go. "That's the problem with an all-consuming occupation, you could say. One day, you're just here alone."

Actually, Hana understood that. She didn't know what she'd do these days without her friends in the village. The wizard cleared his throat, the sound echoing down the stone stairs. Perhaps she'd stayed long enough. Her neck hurt, really, from looking up at the man this way. She glanced back at the door.

She heard him take another step down the stairs, and she turned back around.

"I'm sorry," he said, "I didn't know I could be heard or seen in the village. I'm in here when it happens, and the windows are small at the top. I didn't want to bother any commoners."

Alright, that was enough. At least now he knew. "Well, I'll be going then." She adjusted the walking stick.

"Would you like to see it?"

"*What?*"

"The experiment!" he stammered. "The experiment! What's been making the wizard dust that you see."

She paused.

"Do you trust me?" His eyes opened wide as he asked it.

Of course she didn't trust him. The wizard was fully what

the laundry girls would call a rando. Yet, there was something in his eyes. Maybe a little wizard dust. She was curious. Or bored. Or it was just a long walk back to the village.

"Certainly," she said. "But—" She waved her hand around to indicate the lack of furniture.

"Oh, not here. Yes, please. Come up." He started to walk, then stopped. Spinning around and almost falling down the stairs, he hopped down to the bottom, then lifted his arm up, signaling her to go first.

"No monsters up there?" She did have to ask.

"No," he answered, arm still raised.

Steadying herself with the stick, she carefully ascended the steep hallway, passing by at least four closed doors at the wizard's direction. Her legs were aching, a burn creeping into their tops.

"This one," he said, as a door, ajar, emerged into view. Pushing it the rest of the way open, she stepped inside.

Now, this room was lovely. Everything she'd expect from a wizard. Round shelves of old books—though she was glad not to see any dust, wizardy or brushable—gleaming metal instruments for measure and weight, a series of glass marbles suspended from tiny strands of thread. And in the middle, a round table, centered with a single metal bowl.

"Is it gold?" she asked. She'd not seen so much gold in all her life. It would buy the village, if anyone in the village could afford the gold. Which they couldn't.

"It is," he said. "Only certain metals work with wizardfire."

"What's wizardfire?"

His lips tightened.

"Oh, what, wizard secrets? When you've brought me up

here? Who would I tell? Now, what's wizardfire?" Hana hadn't climbed those stairs for nothing.

"It's the key to wizardry. For a fire wizard."

She thought it was funny that Rain was a fire wizard, but that wasn't an appropriate thing to say. "Is it regular fire?" she asked instead. "Like with a flint?"

"Yes and no," he said. With an apologetic shrug, he added, "It's quite complicated."

She rolled her eyes. "Well, fine, then. But what's the bowl?"

"It's a portal," he said. "An ancient item; I didn't craft it. Yet I've been working with it, understanding it over a very long time. And I'm so close. So close." His last words trailed to a whisper.

"It does require wizardfire to light."

"Yes, I've seen that." Did he not remember why she'd come?

"I just meant you can only stay on your own permission. It could be dangerous."

"I trust you, remember?"

At that, he almost smiled, then his mouth turned back. "Some wizards look down on those who find magic in what already exists. Only crafting is the true art, they say. I disagree. Finding magic in the world that we have, it is a much more powerful force."

She'd said something similar just the other day, but then, she supposed, she hadn't been to wizards' school. Was it a school? But Rain was rubbing his hands.

"So what is it? What's the object you've found?" He'd mentioned the bowl, but the bowl had been crafted by a wizard. She had a sense it was something more.

"A diary."

"A diary?"

"Yes." Glancing at her one last time, as if assessing if he could truly trust the stranger, he lifted from beneath the table a small, gilded book. "Here." His eyes nervous, he offered it to her, almost as if he'd jerk it back if she tried to touch it.

Yet, when she reached for the volume, he only twitched a little, as she nestled it into her wrinkled hands.

"It's empty," she said, paging through the weathered pages.

"Yes, it's been enchanted. I don't think it's truly a crafted item, but an old journal—one that was once ordinary. Perhaps one wizard found it, filled with the sadness of another. He read it, I could imagine, then erased it, readying it to take the wizard's own words. The next wizard, I've surmised, sensed this, and did the same. Over the centuries," he paused, "I only wonder how many stories it has heard."

Not stories, she thought. Journals rarely held stories. She turned the book in her hands, before handing it back to Rain. His own version, she understood, was blank. It was too personal a question to ask. "What do you do with it?"

He set the book into the bowl, whispering as with reverence. "It has seen so many lives, I found it a unique focus for my own enchantments. By coaxing it, I have started to touch the fibers of our being. Of what was, and what could be."

This was getting all too wizardy. "You're going to have to explain it plainer than that."

"I'll show you," he whispered. "If you'd . . . hold my hand?"

She saw no harm in it, reaching for the wizard's hand. For a moment, she stared at their interlocked fingers, each a different tone yet joined in their wrinkles and scars.

"You want to do this?"

She almost laughed. What would they do? But now she was entirely curious. "Yes," she said, adding a reassuring nod.

Slowly, the wizard began an incantation, and above them, a small flame started to rise above the objects. She could not understand, but she started to understand. The fire was not the burning of matter, but something deeper. She sensed she could run her hand through it, and it would not burn her. But not knowing Rain's plan, she had no reason to interrupt.

Instead, she watched.

His eyes stayed fixed like steel while his free hand trembled, hovering over the book as the flame danced above it.

And nothing happened.

Yet, he held still—as still as his trembling hand would allow him—and so Hana waited. And whereas a few minutes before, she'd had no need to see magic, now she found herself not wanting the man to be embarrassed. She smiled, remembering the time Guordji had finally unveiled the nameday cake, just to find her daughter had eaten it.

Distracted by her thoughts, she almost didn't notice the change. For where she had not noticed the thin gold chain around the man's wrist, her gaze caught on its slight flicker. She leaned forward, peering, trying to see what had replaced it. Perhaps steel thread, or clipped maille, or loops of twine.

With a gasp, he lowered his hand, his fingers continuing to tremble. Letting go of her hand with the other, he pushed the robe's sleeve forward, covering the gold chain. "That, I'd not seen before. It was on me. So close to me." He spoke the words to her, but it was almost as if she weren't there.

His head snapped up. "The key is to focus on the blankness

of the pages." Then, she supposed, that's why he hadn't written in the book.

"I saw it," she said, pointing to his wrist.

"You did! I wasn't sure. It's not sight though," he corrected. "It's more than that. I believe a person without eyesight would experience the same sensation."

Hana was unable to deny her growing curiosity. Awareness without sight did not surprise her, but an object *changing* before her eyes was extraordinary. Of course things changed, she corrected. But they did not usually change back.

"Are they changing," she asked, "or is it more like . . . a dream?"

"It is a little like a dream," he mused, "but the object does not change. We only see it differently." His mouth twisted like there was more to it than that. He'd called the bowl a portal. Or, perhaps, the book. Did he believe, then, that they were traveling to a place where the object was different?

"By Martenia," she whispered.

"They are such complex questions," he continued. "I've studied this all my life, and changing a bauble is all I've done." He looked sadly at his arm, then upward to meet her gaze.

Without warning, the wizardfire sparked, in orange, and then blue, and Hana reached forward to grasp the table as the room shifted around them.

All at once, Rain's face was shaven bare, but only quickly as his beard popped back into place. He was wearing an apron, and then not, and then her own hands changed, with fewer wrinkles and the scars smoothed away.

The tower was there, and then it was a meadow, and then the forest trees blinked in and out around them. A vastness of water, wider than the sky. A ship, with sails billowing in the wind. And Rain, wearing a stained jacket, his face filled with fear as he seemed desperately trying to grasp something.

And this was all too much for Hana on a Monday, and so she closed it off, and with a thud the wizardfire snapped out, shooting upward in a white streak, and they were back in the tower, just as they had been. Rain blinked.

"By Martenia!" Hana shouted, stepping back away. "Now that was plenty." As she tried to gather herself, she realized that above them, the tower must be popping and burping the dark clouds over the valley. In here, she could not sense them. "I implore you to stop disturbing the village," she sputtered, remembering that was why she was here in the first place.

Yet could she? Could she ask this man to stop his work, after what she'd just seen? "At least be considerate," she said in a softer tone. "Know that we sleep in the night, and that night watchers sleep in the day, and that we have the desire to look up and see the sunny day or watch the rain clouds pass." She stopped.

"You know, your work isn't all the issue." Wasn't it? Wasn't it the only issue? "We don't know you," she blurted. "Maybe you could walk to the village sometime. Or . . . fly." Couldn't wizards fly? "Port." That sounded sarcastic, so she shifted. "Get a haircut, or I mean, a trim, I mean, it's your deal." She shouldn't have brought up his beard. She was just so *flustered*. How big was that lake?

Rain was still just standing there, as if he had more to say but couldn't bring himself to say it. "That was powerful," was all he finally muttered.

Pausing, he added, "In one of the visions, I saw a female wizard. Perhaps you could—"

Hana snorted. She didn't mean to, but that was funny. "Of course there are female wizards. You don't need a vision for that. If men are doing it, women are doing it too! You just don't have them in your school. Or, if you do, you call them men. No," she confirmed, picking her walking stick from where it had clattered to the floor, "I'm fine as I am."

She nearly tripped, as her legs wobbled unsteadily. With a breath, she shook each leg, glad to see they seemed willing to again obey her.

"Who's Martenia?"

Martenia? Had she said that? "Nothing you need to know about."

He grinned, giving her a slight nod. "My apologies. It's just—" He pointed toward the table. Yes, she understood, the experience had been rather familiar.

"Well, I should be going. It's a long walk down and I intend to enjoy it."

"That's nice," he said. "Do you need anything?"

Her bag was still slung over her shoulder. "No. I do not." She didn't mean to be rude, but, well, *really*.

"Then, safe travels. And thank you for telling me about the village."

"Of course." So, then, he'd try to watch his wizardfire. Smiling, she turned to leave.

"Hana?"

She turned back around.

"If I go there, could we talk? You and I?"

Did he really? Well, she thought, why not. Maybe there's a first time for everything.

"Only in *this* world," she said with a grin. She glanced one more moment at the table with the golden bowl and the empty book.

And she walked back out onto the path.

Bus Stops

This was written in 2017 for a friend's publication—It was my first year back in Michigan, and I was enjoying taking the bus down Woodward (yes, I know it's named for a dude, not a direction, but I liked it here) into the city. I wanted to share that joy, and I wrote this light-hearted piece. The publication wasn't able to be completed, so maybe I can share this joy now.

I'M waiting for the bus and I'm standing at the stop and the people say hello as they gather on the block
The bus is not on time but the lady from the shop says she didn't see it stop
So we're probably just fine

Red Light
Green Light
Loud Brakes
Stop

Please - go ahead

Door shuts, doesn't wait
Pull my bills out, slide them straight
Woodward, Cityward, we're anyward but stayward

One step two step buy the ticket we depart
Seats up in the higher part

Headphones stare the other way
Smiles say how is your day
Swing around
To find a seat
Bus is on its way

Hi, Hello
Where do you go
The city's fine
Enjoy your time
And here's a place
Where I spend mine
My stop is there
But you take care
Enjoy it there or anywhere
Off she goes
At even pace
Another rider takes her place
Next stop
Two stops
Pull the rope
For our stop
The weather's fine
It's always fine
Ding the stop now off we hop

On the walk, now where am I?
The bus already flying by
Goodbye smiles
Goodbye friends
Peace to where your journey ends

We stop and look around with the cool air on our breath

One foot in front of the other
It's a perfect day to get out and enjoy life

And I am happy to be here among friends and with things I'd
like to do

Bagels

This piece was written for a 2015 anthology *Call of the Warrior* by the now closed small press, one that was notably early in the modern indie press world, Read Write Muse. I am proud that my first published short work took the theme of warrior and made it about fighting emotional violence and standing up for others with less privilege. I hope you enjoy.

"Now, what's this next one?" Mr. Knutsen inquired. "*Lactation room?* Is that—" Somewhere in the executive's mind, an alarm triggered regarding legally sensitive subjects. He tapped the table. "Oh, yes, a mothers room. Whoever submitted this may not be aware that we already have one."

Louise stared down at her pristine yellow binder. She had stayed late several evenings working on this proposal. "Mr. Knutsen, I authored this one myself. It's a change from what we have and I'd like to present it."

He reached for his coffee. "Not sure I understand. It doesn't seem like something, with your level of experience, that would impact you."

Experience was the preferred euphemism for *old*, as there was no law for experience discrimination. A pit formed in her chest. Within twenty seconds, he had turned to evaluate Louise rather than her proposal.

"No, I'm not pregnant," she answered in level tones, "nor should we start rumors of my experience." Mr. Knutsen's face tightened and his deputy pursed her lips. Around the table, several people averted their eyes. "You don't need to require a thing in order to recommend it, of course. For example, you approved the smoking shelter though Mrs. Knutsen told everyone at the picnic that you had quit."

Mr. Knutsen huffed, shaking his head at the comparison. "Of course that's not for me. You can't have people standing in the rain; it isn't right. That's just looking out for people. Now, back to this . . . mothers room, who's complaining about it?"

I am not bringing her into this. Louise gestured toward Mr. Knutsen's binder. "The current space is in the restroom; my proposal details an update that would provide a more welcoming environment for lactating employees."

Mr. Knutsen forced a smile. "It's not *in* the bathroom; it's a separate area with a divider. I know of only one person affected, and she has been fairly accommodated, in full compliance with the law. We looked up the requirements."

The planning lead nodded his head in agreement.

"Perhaps I could approve a sign," Mr. Knutsen offered, "to place outside. That would show we have a family-friendly environment."

Louise took a deep breath, reminding herself this wasn't on her mind, either, until last month. After a lunchtime bowl of chili, she was hoping she could sneak away for "a couple of things," as her husband referred to it. As she walked into the stall she heard an unusual sound, muffled, from behind an industrial-looking separator.

Zzzz. Zzzz. Zzzz. It took her a moment to place the sound. *Oh, a breast pump!*

She liked how times had changed; attitudes had been so different when her own children were born. She winced, remembering the comments people had made about her returning to work at all, and the years she had smiled back despite the wounds inside. Surely they didn't need to use the restroom for pumping milk. *And I came in here to—* Louise left, her business unfinished.

She had hesitated to approach the young woman, but the situation nagged at her mind. It must have been Tanya from accounting. She had returned not long ago from maternity leave, a new picture of a tiny baby boy on her desk. "Let me know if you need anything," people had remarked, before returning to their email.

"Tanya?" Louise had inquired after ensuring they were alone. "If you don't mind me asking, does it bother you to have to use the restroom to pump?"

The look on Tanya's face showed her true feelings, but she appeared reticent to answer.

"I'm sorry; I didn't mean to pry," Louise responded, turning to leave.

"I hate it," the young woman whispered, turning Louise in mid-stride. "I can't relax with people *peeing* in the background. And there's no lock; I'm always scared someone's going to walk in."

"Have you said anything?"

Tanya shook her head. "I don't want to bring it up; I draw enough attention as it is. They're always staring at my bag in meetings, wondering if I'll have to leave. If I complained about the room, it would just remind them that I have no business being here anyway. That's what they think."

"You don't know that," Louise answered, doubting the words as she spoke them. "You could give them a chance. The fiscal year planning meeting is coming up. You could submit it."

"I'm not talking to them about my . . . *breasts*. I'll make it work."

Louise stifled a grin. "Tanya, despite your perceptions of the executive staff, I assure you they have all encountered breasts in their time. Even Mr. Knutsen."

Tanya chuckled. "Maybe."

For days, Tanya's situation continued to rankle Louise, until sitting at her keyboard with an evening cup of rooibos tea, she began to draw up the requirements: a comfortable chair, a desk, outlets, a fridge, a clock, a locking door, a bulletin board, and a sink—along with a concise justification for each. *There*, she had finally declared, as she punched holes into the side of the proposal.

She stared at the binder now, the extra copies in front of her. Louise opened her mouth to protest, but Mr. Knutsen had already moved on to approving construction of a new shelf in the snack area, strong enough to hold full toaster ovens rather than traditional vertical toasters.

"Thanks for everyone's input," Mr. Knutsen was saying. "All great improvements for our team. We've got another set to get through, but I need a bio-break first. Let's take ten."

The executives filed from the room as an administrative assistant bumped past with large bags of bagels. The planning lead was following behind. "Everything bagels are my favorite," he explained. Louise responded with a polite smile as she walked past the table and out into the hallway.

Louise stepped into the restroom and found herself staring at the dividing wall with resentment. The pit now weighed heavy inside her. It wasn't that she had been dismissed; it certainly wasn't the first time. It was the idea of young people afraid to raise their voices and no one coming to their aid.

She walked into the small space. It was bare except for an office chair, a small folding table, and a picture of Tanya's boy pinned to the wall. A toilet flushed in the background. *They think they can put us away. That things will return to how they were.*

She didn't want to wait for next year's review; every year would be another woman made to feel dirty and unwelcome in her own place of work. She ran her hands across the table, and a terrible idea sprang to mind. *I wouldn't. Would I?*

Louise stepped back into the hallway and nearly walked right into Mr. Knutsen emerging from the other side, tossing a paper towel into the can as the door swung closed behind him.

"Louise, don't take it wrong. We can't accommodate every niche need or there wouldn't be resources to keep the lights on." He reached toward her shoulder, stopping short as if held back by an invisible lawyer.

"I just worry, Sir, that younger parents won't be drawn to work here. It would be a shame to lose some really talented people over a change that would be easy for us to make."

Mr. Knutsen nodded. "Louise, I know you well enough to know that you won't take this the wrong way, but what if they do leave? Aren't their families better off? Why would we stand in the way of mothers spending more time with their children?" His hand patted the air.

Years of painful memories hit Louise in the chest as Mr. Knutsen walked back into the room.

Louise made up her mind.

As she walked into the room, everyone was absorbed into their phones, including Mr. Knutsen. They ignored her completely as they finished their emails or made a quick call home, giving her time to slip from the room.

She sat back into her seat as Mr. Knutsen finally looked up from his phone. "Everyone, help yourself to some—" he started, staring at the table to the side, covered with a series of neatly arranged papers. "Where are the bagels?" He turned with a pointed finger to his deputy. "Didn't Tracy bring in the bagels, Melanie?" Melanie peered at the table in confusion.

Louise braced herself and raised a hand. "I needed room to set out my proposal so that everyone could review, since no one had the chance to read it earlier. I moved the bagels to the ladies room."

Mr. Knutsen's face burned red, and his deputy squinted. The planning lead glanced suspiciously at his everything bagel. To his left, a man's eyes opened wide, and another gaped to his right. The man across the table glanced away, making a face of disgust.

A quick flash of doubt filled Louise before being pushed away by resolve. *Too late now. If I just got myself fired, I'll go out fighting.* "There's no need for concern. I set them out behind the divider, so they aren't technically in the ladies room. It's very clean there."

That afternoon, Louise watched for a chance to catch Tanya alone. "The planning meeting was today. A pumping room—it's on the list."

Tanya stepped back. "Wow, really?"

Her eyes clouded, a reaction Louise didn't expect.

"I'm sorry; did I go too far? I didn't think you'd—"

"No," Tanya waved her hand. "No, please. I'm just surprised, is all. Nobody's ever fought for me before. Not here, anyway."

Louise clutched the binder. "This was only the first round. We still have to get it past the V.P."

"It doesn't matter. Just that you tried, well, it means so much to me. Thank you."

"Hang in there. I'm not ready to give up." Louise met Tanya's eyes for a moment. "Everyone makes tough choices. Don't let them get to you."

"I'll remember that." With a final nod, Tanya hefted the bag's thick strap onto her shoulder and headed toward the restroom.

Pod Train

In May 2020, I saw a prompt for a short fiction contest with a $1000 prize, based on the question to "imagine ways that technology can improve how we relate to each other and bring us closer, even across species." It was like, wait, a fiction contest where vegan perspectives might be valued? I felt I had to try. I was still recovering from my mental collapse just weeks before, and still on heavy medication; it was a particularly rough time. Given all that, and given this was the first thing I wrote after being scared that maybe I couldn't write again—I am very proud of this piece. Of note, the contest welcomed POVs from other species, and while I'd written non-human POVs before (the newts of *Diamondsong* being a recent one), I decided to take a risk and write a story that shifts between omni and multiple 3rd person POVs. I felt that by doing so, I could really emphasize the connection aspect, and I could de-center the humans while not romanticizing a non-human by making them communicate on human terms. I was also at the time very concerned about the surge of overt white supremacy in our government and culture—even though this was written just before the murder of George Floyd and subsequent protests, it's important to keep on the record that movements against race disparities in America were already broiling at that time. So while I wouldn't presume to frame a story this way, in my mind this was also an Afrofuturism and Indigenous Futurisms story and any other genres that portray each of our authenticity existing and being respected in a future world. A world striving for equality; what better aspect to connect technology with the total lack of it. A goal for all and always. Again, I'm very proud of this little story—and hope you enjoy. The most recent story of the collection and one with hope, compassion, and futurisms in mind, it felt like the right one on which to end.

Thank you, so much, for reading this collection.

SHE scrambled over the marbled river rocks, a tart scent sharp on her nose. She was growing tired, but a nice bite of fruit would settle her. The sweetness of the juice stayed on her mind as she bounded up the hill, weaving through the brush and jumping over felled boughs—until other senses stopped her.

The rumble of the long shiny thing, far in the distance. In her paws, her ears.

This time, she would go meet it. The long shiny thing never bothered her, not like the round shiny things that floated and watched with spots and knobs, like giant shiny bees. One of those poked her once, when she was trying to sleep. She got a good swipe back at it, but then it flew away. She hoped that taught it not to bother her.

The long shiny thing was much nicer. Even when she was sleeping, its rumble would enter her dreams, a little like the rumble of kits. It went on its way, and did not try and find her.

She bounded through the trees, toward the clearing. Sometimes, the long shiny thing's kits would visit, then be carried away again. She liked seeing them.

Clambering up to the branches of a tree, she crunched into a young fruit, peering out as the glint of the long shiny thing curved through the forest.

A dark set of lines guided it, like fish unable to leave a stream. Rounded pods of different sizes stuck to the center like grapes, each with humans inside: some were gazing outward, others resting, and others tapping on their screens.

As the train swung past, one of the small pods separated, and slid away, slowing as it moved with graceful stillness down the curving side track, and finally coming to a full and silent stop in the early morning light. With the train now quiet, the other sounds stepped back into place. Some birds flapped away from the trees, and others swooped near and then away. Back at the river, slick otters splashed, and a heron soared up and toward the pod, landing on a boulder. Thin, dark feathers pointed back and away from a long, gray and yellow beak, and scruffy plumage spread out, across the bird's back and down a curved, mottled neck.

From the pod, a young child pressed up against the glass, watching as the heron flapped away and back into the trees.

Nearby, a middle-aged human grinned. The pod screens showed the same images, but he too preferred the window. "It feels different in person," he said.

It had been a while since he'd taken the train to Detroit, and he was looking forward to seeing the city. He'd grown up in the video era, of course, but there was something about feeling the breeze on your face and smelling the streetside pizza—Detroit pizza was different than Chicago pizza, not just in the shallower pans but in their preference for beet cheeses—that reminded him he was alive. Which was exactly why they were here.

The doorlock clicked.

"So here's the vista," he said, the words feeling inadequate. The door slid open, and they stepped out onto the circular platform, a nearly invisible hard mesh separating them from the expanses of Biome N-048. Arborland, as the locals called it.

The child and father stretched and walked over to the platform edge, drinking in the symphony around them. Swaying leaves, meandering water, and the chirps and creaks and hops and jumps of small animals in the trees, the water, and the air.

"They're getting taller," the father mentioned, smiling up at the waving treetops, a deep purple line of lace against the post-dawn sky.

The child rushed around the platform's edge. "What's that? In that tree? Something gray and furry!"

The man fumbled for his phone, clicking a few times then peering through. "That's a fox. I don't know more; I turned off analysis. Oh, but look, here they come."

He slid the phone into his pocket as the creature jumped to a lower branch and then backed down the trunk, not taking her eyes off of the two humans. Slowly, she walked toward them.

The child was entranced, and pressed both hands against the mesh.

Dad was speaking again. "You'll see all sorts of different animals in the biomes than you would in the panomes. Here, we have huge birds, foxes, wolves, even bears." He paused. "In other parts of the world, the animals are even larger. They've restored herds of real elephants, large cats. Giraffes, taller than you could imagine." Dad shook his head and raised his hand upward, with that dreamy look he often got. "But I like it here. I like seeing the squirrels and chipmunks. Jay? What do you think?"

"I like the fox," Jay replied. "There are squirrels and chipmunks in Chicago." They would run around in the trees outside the playground, hopping and bouncing.

"I know," Dad said, "but I like seeing them here."

The fox crept closer, looking almost like they were curious. "Hello," Jay whispered. "Good morning." The fox cocked their head in response.

Delighted, Jay wanted to stare out at the fox forever, but

there were so many questions piling up. "So we really just leave everything alone here? You know, the trees and the plants and the animals?" They talked about the biomes all the time in school, but it was never really clear about how they *worked*.

Dad shook his head, the wistful look fading. "It's not so simple anymore. Nothing has been simple since humanity built its first tools. We try to minimize intervention, but we also need to look out for the preservation of species. The planet as a whole. Balance."

"I thought nature made balance." Teacher always said that.

"It does. Issue is, humans are nature too. Look, it gets complicated. Diet, birth control, violence reduction, synth flesh, fire and flood. Complicated issues that we'll be debating for centuries, I think."

"That sounds like a lot of work for just having nature." Something jarred in that. "Wait. If there's no people in the biomes then who runs them?"

Dad chuckled. "What a human way to put that. First, there are *some* people in the biomes, and in the way that you mean it, they are administered by the Core Nations."

Oh. "But I thought the Core Nations lived in the panomes."

"Yes, they do. They also run several panomes. Hey," Dad shifted and gave Jay *that look*. "I'll be happy to explain this all once we're back on the train, but while we're here, let's just watch. Look, that fox sure is interested in you."

Jay sat down, trying to leave the questions for later. The fox walked closer and was almost up to the mesh. They sniffed. Jay noticed the details of their wet, dark nose. The way the white chin fur blended upward into stripes of gray that met like a star in between their ears. Long whiskers that never stayed still, and glowing, dark brown eyes with the richness of polished wood but with the knowing gaze of a whole universe. How could something so beautiful be real?

The sound of human talking ceased, and the fox breathed, the sweet apple juice still running in her mouth. The man stayed standing, hands on his hips, gazing out at something farther away than an apple tree or even a river. And his child sat, silently, eyes locked with the furry gray fox, who sat back on the moss, legs curling underneath.

Time passed by, unmeasured. The light grew, and a cloud appeared, and a soft beep sounded from within the man's pocket.

He sighed. "Maybe we can stop again on the way back but I want to get to the meeting with time to prepare. It's going to be wonderful to see everyone in person." The last part was murmured as if to himself. "It's been a minute." He clicked something on his phone.

Slowly, Jay rose and stepped back into the pod. "I can't wait to see Detroit," a lilting voice echoed from inside.

The man smiled, for once a broad, careless smile. "Maybe we'll see you again," he said to the fox, who turned and darted away, bounding back into the forest. A striped chipmunk appeared nearby, shaking a tiny tail, and the man's mouth twitched.

He stepped back inside. The pod doors closed, and the air handler circled, creating a rush of air around them and a poof of microscopic mist. An orange light switched to green. The motor whirred.

The pod climbed up the long curve back to the main track, with two human faces visible in the curved glass windows. And when it sped away, toward the gently rising sun, beyond the trees and the birds, gleaming black towers emerged into view, the morning sun beaming down onto sleek surfaces and tailored parks. Onto a city grown tall from strength, truth, resilience, and hope itself. Some of the greatest innovations the world had ever seen came from the Detroit panome, not just before the revolution, but turning the wheels to create it.

Other Works

There are more stories that I'm proud of during this time-frame, and regarding which, I will direct you to their original publication:

"The New Year's Buzz" (2017) and **"Alyri"** (2018) on Every Day Fiction.

"Tragedia" (2018) in my own *As Told by Things*. This is my true masterpiece of flash fiction. The time someone told me they loved it at a panel was . . . so cool.

"What I See" (2018) also in *As Told by Things*. Very fond of this sweet story told by the comic convention bathroom mirror.

"Sigrun is Not Here" (2019) in my own *Five Minutes at Hotel Stormcove*. I was in a mood with this piece.

"Duality" (2019) in Mad Scientist Journal's *I Didn't Break the Lamp*, edited by Jeremy Zimmerman and Dawn Zimmerman. A story of imaginary friends, truth, and love.

"Optimization" (2019) in *Space Opera Libretti*, edited by Jennifer Lee Rossman and Brian McNett. This, my first Space Opera, is filled with fun and acceptance and music and glam.

Classified Ad: **"NEEDED: Magic Dissolution Expert"** in *Mad Scientist Journal, Winter 2020*.

"Ink" (2020) in my own *Community of Magic Pens*. I've gone through a lot this year, and this little flash piece is so close to me.

"Petition" (2020) in Queer Sci Fi's *Innovation*. This was especially fun as I needed to write an entire fantasy story in less than 300 words while meeting three criteria: a clear arc (not a vignette), visible queer representation, and the theme of innovation.

"Hetta, who is plain" (2020). This was written for the 2020 Origins Library Anthology, a book which never materialized after the event was cancelled. I hope to see it in the 2021 book, but either way, keep an eye out for this story, as I really love it.

I hope you will check out these lovely collections.

About the Author

E.D.E. Bell (she/e) loves fantasy fiction and enjoys blending classic and modern elements. A passionate vegan and earnest progressive, she feels strongly about issues related to equality and compassion. Her works often explore conceptions of identity and community, including themes of friendship, family, and connection. She lives in Ferndale, Michigan, where she writes stories and revels in garlic. You can follow her adventures at edebell.com.

Bell was born in the year of the fire dragon during a Cleveland blizzard. After a youth in the Mitten, an MSE in Electrical Engineering from the University of Michigan, three wonderful children, and nearly two decades in Northern Virginia and Southwest Ohio developing technical intelligence strategy, she, with her beloved spouse, started the indie press Atthis Arts. Working through mental disorders and an ever-complicated world, she now tries to bring light and love as she can through fantasy fiction, as a proud part of the Detroit arts community.

www.ingramcontent.com/pod-product-compliance
Lightning Source LLC
Chambersburg PA
CBHW021146190726
48288CB00008B/2844